A QUESTION OF DIGNITY

"We should never allow a disease process define our dignity. — Shiela

A QUESTION OF DIGNITY

A SOCIETY DYING
FOR THE ANSWER

SHEILA D. HOLT

TATE PUBLISHING & Enterprises

Published by Tate Publishing & Enterprises, LLC
127 E. Trade Center Terrace | Mustang, Oklahoma 73064 USA
1.888.361.9473 | www.tatepublishing.com

Tate Publishing is committed to excellence in the publishing industry. The company reflects the philosophy established by the founders, based on Psalm 68:11,
"The Lord gave the word and great was the company of those who published it."

Book design copyright © 2009 by Tate Publishing, LLC. All rights reserved.
Cover design by Tyler Evans
Interior design by Blake Brasor

Published in the United States of America

ISBN: 978-1-60799-445-9
1. Fiction, Legal
2. Social Science, Death & Dying
09.05.27

ACKNOWLEDGMENTS

My mother, Joann Scott, who is now resting peacefully in the hands of our Lord Jesus Christ, is the sole inspiration for this book. I dedicate this book to my grandmother, Eleanor Sides, who traveled the long road of Alzheimer's disease and taught me how to love and live life to the fullest.

A special appreciation is given to my husband, David, who encouraged and supported me throughout the process of writing and editing this book.

A deep and heartfelt appreciation is offered to Tate Publishing. To work with Christian brothers and sisters is truly a dream come true.

To my children, Rusty, Rachel, and Peter, I wish to extend my deepest appreciation for their constant love and support.

For my friends Norma Spalding, Cindy Piper, Dan and Karen Hufford, and Kelly and Sue Richlin, who took such genuine interest in the value of my book from the beginning to the end; I will never forget our special friendship.

I

Henry lay stiffly in the hospital bed. He turned his head and looked out the large window. The scene outside reflected the mood in Henry's room. It was midmorning in Portland, Oregon, but the sky was dark. Rain fell quietly outside Henry's room, still more audible than the tears flowing down his cheeks. It was a gloomy day and would be the last for Henry Glass.

Seventy-nine-year-old Henry had been diagnosed with Alzheimer's disease two years before. If Henry had been able to, he might have been reminiscing about recently living with his daughter, Judy. Before that, Henry had lived alone in a comfortable home, once occupied by his family. Henry's wife,

Eva, had died ten years earlier. Her death nearly devastated Henry, for in his mind they shared a near-perfect marriage.

In earlier years Henry had worked as an accountant for a large produce company. He had always felt blessed and tried to enjoy life to the fullest. Now Henry's world was filled with confusion.

His daughter did her best to care for her father and her own family, but the past several months had taken their toll. She was mentally and physically exhausted. At his last doctor's appointment Henry's physician had recommended Peaceful Transitions to Judy and her brother, Mike.

The unpaved road leading to Peaceful Transitions was serene and wound deep into the woods that surrounded the huge Southern Colonial-period mansion. Judy's first impression was of Southern comfort. The architecture seemed to invite quiet contemplation.

Indeed, patients who entered the gates of Peaceful Transitions soon found their final resting place because this classic Southern mansion served as the nation's first legalized euthanasia clinic.

Henry awaited his destiny, his children at his side. Mike stood near the foot of the bed, and Judy gripped Henry's right hand. Henry's left arm lay by his side while an IV fluid dripped slowly into his vein. Judy's palm was sweaty, and she was unaware of the classical music that permeated the room.

The door to Henry's room inched open, and Dr. William McKay, the director of Peaceful Transitions, entered.

Dr. McKay had begun his career as a general practitioner

some thirty years ago. Judy turned toward him and noticed that he stood about six feet tall, had an athletic build, and looked to be in his sixties. His curly salt-and-pepper hair agreed with his distinguished features. Judy thought he made the perfect PR person to lead such a facility until she glanced into his gray eyes.

They gave the impression of a haughty, distant man. Dr. McKay reached into his pocket and pulled out a full syringe.

"Hello, Henry. You look very peaceful. In a few minutes, I'll begin the medication. I want you to relax and just listen to the music," said Dr. McKay. He checked Henry's IV and assured himself that everything was in proper working order.

As the syringe entered the IV port, Henry turned toward his daughter with a sad, vacant look.

Judy smiled through her tears and said, "Dad, you've lived a good, long life. It's time for you to rest and be with Mom again."

Mike moved closer to Judy, hugging her at their father's side. "We have to let you go now, Dad. It's for the best. We love you."

As Dr. McKay depressed the plunger on the syringe, Henry's eyes closed. A single tear flowed from his eye as his breathing gradually slowed, then stopped.

2

At the headquarters of *Situational Life* Magazine in Phoenix, Arizona, Rachel Scott was working diligently on her latest assignment.

She enjoyed working at the family-oriented magazine, whose topics included a myriad of life situations, from wedding planning to funeral arrangements. Rachel Scott was one of the magazine's top journalists.

Rachel, who had been born in Carmel, California, was drawn to journalism from an early age. During her junior high years, she worked on the yearbook staff. In high school, she was the editor of the Carmel High School Yearbook and even started her own school newspaper. Her good grades and creative drive landed her at Stanford University, where she excelled in investigative journalism.

It was at Stanford that Rachel met her future husband, Kyle. Kyle had planned on becoming a doctor, but by the end of his freshman year he realized the healing profession wasn't his calling.

What Kyle really loved was history; old books on any kind of history. He was intrigued by wars, Civil Rights movements, economic shifts, and historical landmarks. He changed his major to education and now chaired the history department at Phoenix Community College.

Rachel was studiously critiquing her recent article on the nation's long-term care crisis when her phone rang. She jerked upright in her chair and grabbed the phone.

"Rachel speaking."

It was Rusty Richlin, her boss. "Hi, Rachel, can you come into my office?"

"Sure, Rusty. I'll be right there."

Rachel closed her file. Once, a dishonest roommate had helped herself to one of Rachel's papers when Rachel had left a file open on her computer. This had cost both of them a visit to the dean's office.

Rusty grinned at Rachel as she entered his office. "How's the story on long-term care going?"

"It's terrible, Rusty. I can't believe there's no long-term-care payment system. I swear I thought Medicare covered long-term care."

"It doesn't?"

"Nope. Most of the elderly depend on the state to cover long-term expenses. And then only if they are low-income."

"I thought people could qualify by getting rid of their assets."

Rachel grimaced. "Yeah, that's pretty humiliating—not to mention illegal."

Rusty pulled open a drawer and took out a file. "So what happens if they need help or a nursing home?"

"Well, considering the average cost of a nursing home is about $60,000 a year, it's a huge problem. If they aren't covered by the state welfare program, they can spend everything real fast." Rachel paused as Rusty absorbed the information. "What else did you need?"

Rusty handed Rachel the file he'd been holding. "I have something else for you. This one might be a little touchy."

"Why? What's up?"

"There's a new clinic in Oregon. It's a euthanasia clinic called Peaceful Transitions."

Rachel's eyes opened wide. "What exactly is that?"

"It's a clinic that ends the suffering of terminally ill people, legally. You know, with flowers and touchy-feely pastel colors, everything a dying person could want. Anyway, see if you can wrap up the long-term care story. The director of Peaceful Transitions is expecting you on Monday."

Here we go again, thought Rachel, but she wasn't surprised by a short-notice assignment. Rachel was adaptable, and Rusty knew it. "I'm not sure I even know where to begin with this. I mean, this clinic actually kills people?"

"I think the idea is, when people reach a certain level of illness, their dignity dwindles down to nothing, and then the euthanasia puts them out of their misery."

"I'm not sure I buy that."

"Well, go figure it out. Then write me a story."

It was already after five thirty, and Rachel was feeling the pressure of putting together a lead story. She knew she wouldn't go to sleep until she was finished, so she stopped for Chinese takeout to give herself more time to write.

She pulled into a driveway at the end of a cul-de-sac in a newer development in Phoenix. She and Kyle had scraped and saved every penny to buy their dream home. Now their kids were in a good neighborhood and went to school in the best district, so they didn't mind their missed nights out or forfeited vacations.

As Rachel pushed through the door into the kitchen, Sarah, Rachel's reserved twelve-year-old, stood back; but Laura, who was eight, quickly moved in for a combination tackle/hug. Rachel reciprocated the hug then scooted past to set down the brown-bagged dinner.

"I had a great day, Mom! My teacher is going to be a clown at the school carnival!" Laura could find joy in the smallest things, and it was impossible not to be affected by her natural exuberance.

On the other hand, Sarah took on the worries of the world. Unlike her sister, she was too afraid of disappointing others or missing an opportunity to help someone to be able to live life in unconfined joy. "Mom, I need to turn in my candy money tomorrow."

"Oh, Sarah, I nearly forgot. Hang on, we'll get it together."

Rachel momentarily escaped her daughters and turned to her sixteen-year-old babysitter, Stacy. "How's life, Stacy?"

Stacy had been their sitter for almost a year. Stacy's mom had been one of the first neighbors to welcome them after they moved in. Rachel felt blessed to have such a positive role model around her girls. Stacy enjoyed books, her church youth group, and of course, boys.

Stacy smiled at Rachel. "I'm doing pretty well, Mrs. Scott. Jake Morris asked me to the prom. Mom and Dad are still deciding if I can go."

"The prom! I can't believe you're already going to a prom! I hope your folks say you can go."

"You and me both!"

Rachel laughed as she set the table and distributed the Chinese food. She watched Stacy pack up her books and again reflected on how lucky she had been to find Stacy. That reminded Rachel that she wanted to ask her a favor.

"I'm going to be out of town on Monday. Could you stay a little later until Kyle gets home?"

"Yeah, no problem." Stacy started toward the door.

Rachel asked, "How're your parents doing?"

"They're great. Mom just started a new job at the bakery. I think she was getting bored at home."

"Well, her pound-cake-making skills alone qualify her for that job! Please tell them hello for me."

Stacy made her way out the door. "I will. Well, I better get going."

"Thanks again for staying late Monday."

"You're welcome, no problem. Have a safe trip, Mrs. Scott."

Stacy began to walk home. She had taken her driver's license test on her sixteenth birthday and passed. Her parents lent her their car whenever they were able.

Rachel watched as Stacy turned the corner and prayed

her daughters would be as agreeable when they hit their teenage years.

Rachel's small working area looked out the window into the backyard. The gigantic master bedroom was one of the features Rachel had fallen in love with when they first saw the house. Rachel knew how lucky she was to be able to combine her work with her family life.

As she was working on her assignment, Kyle tried to sneak up on her, but at the last minute she spun around and said, "Boo! Dinner is in the fridge. I already ate with the girls. Sorry, but I've got a deadline."

"No problem. When's your deadline?" Kyle bent over to greet Rachel with a kiss.

"Tomorrow. I've got to fly to Oregon on Monday. I'm writing a story about a euthanasia clinic."

"A what clinic?"

Rachel smiled as she answered, "Euthanasia; I'm not exactly sure what it's all about."

"Sounds Kevorkianish."

"Could be," said Rachel.

One of the things that had drawn Rachel to Kyle was his sense of humor. He took life with a grain of salt and could almost always find humor in anything. Tonight was no exception.

"How sick do you have to be to go? Maybe we could send your mom!"

"Very funny!"

"You've heard that Kevorkian joke, haven't you?"

"Do I want to?"

Kyle sat down and twirled the leather chair so Rachel was facing him. "Okay, so Kevorkian is standing in front of a judge. The judge said, 'You're guilty.' Kevorkian said, 'Well, Judge, if it's the death penalty, I'd rather do it myself.'"

Rachel giggled. "You're a sick man." She leaned over the bed, grabbed a pillow, and threw it at Kyle. "You've really missed your calling. You should have been a stand-up comedian."

Kyle strutted toward the doorway. "I know. I'm starving."

"All kidding aside, I have to admit I'm a little nervous about this story."

"How come?"

"I guess because I'm not sure what to expect. I remember when Oregon voted to legalize euthanasia, but I never heard about any specific clinics. Or maybe I did hear about it but just blocked it out. It seems kind of creepy. Anyway, go eat some dinner."

"Okay."

Rachel sat in her chair planning her trip to Oregon. She pulled up the weather on her computer and decided her boots and sweaters were coming for the trip. Laura and Sarah ran into the room and crawled onto the king-sized bed. She glanced over and saw her two daughters sitting on the bed, staring with doleful eyes.

Laura was fidgeting with her latest Barbie's hair and asked, "Where are you going, Mama?"

"Oregon."

Sarah turned over on the bed and stared at the ceiling. "How far is Oregon?"

Rachel sensed Sarah's worry and decided to give her an answer to put her at ease. "Close enough to call my cell phone anytime you want to."

Laura leaped off the bed. "Really?"

"Absolutely!"

Sarah rolled her eyes. "She has free long-distance calling. It's not that big of a deal. Mama, is this a good story?"

"I'm not sure, honey."

"Well, is it a happy story or a sad story?"

Rachel looked at her eldest daughter and realized how mature she was becoming. "I imagine it depends on who's telling the story."

Laura smiled brightly and said, "You're telling the story! I want it to be a happy story!"

Sarah agreed. "Me too."

Rachel agreed and hugged her two daughters.

Rachel glanced up as she fastened the airplane seatbelt. She took the proffered pillow and thanked the airline attendant. She hated early-morning flights, especially during weekdays. She worried about Kyle making breakfast and getting the girls to school on time. Rachel's biggest demon was her C-personality: what she called the *caregiver syndrome*.

Ever since Rachel had been little, she felt driven to take care of everyone and everything. She didn't have faith enough to let things happen as they may. This was something Rachel was aware of and in recent months a project she had been focused on.

Rachel sighed as she opened her purse. She retrieved her wallet and pulled out a picture of her grandfather. He was wearing a military uniform from World War II. Rachel smiled as she remembered her love for Grandpa James. She dug farther into her purse and pulled out a business card Rusty had given her on Friday.

Rachel noted the clinic's name, Peaceful Transitions, and the director's name, Dr. Bill McKay. At the bottom of the card it read, *Ending Life with Dignity*.

Rachel reflected on that line as her attention returned to the picture in her other hand.

3

Rachel was sitting in the lobby at Peaceful Transitions. Her head was still reeling from the beauty of the entrance into the facility. She had somehow felt as if she were entering a scene on the set of *Gone with the Wind*. The reception area reminded her of a grand hotel lobby.

"Hello, Ms. Scott. I'm Dr. McKay, the director of Peaceful Transitions." Standing before her was a well-dressed man who happened to be wearing more jewelry than Rachel had in her whole jewelry box. Dr. McKay extended his right hand to Rachel.

Rachel extended her hand. "Pleasure to meet you Dr. McKay. Please call me Rachel."

"All right, Rachel. I'm sure you have a lot of questions, but I'd like to start out with a tour of the facility."

"That would be great. I appreciate you taking this time for me."

Dr. McKay stopped walking and spoke directly to Rachel. "No, I am the one who appreciates your time, Ms. Scott."

Rachel was about to correct Dr. McKay and remind him to call her Rachel, but something about the way he was looking at her stopped her. She felt frozen, and everything in her wanted to run out the front door. She quickly glanced away from Dr. McKay and decided to avoid eye contact with him from then on. *What is it about this man?* It didn't make sense to Rachel how a man with his job description could leave one so ill at ease. *I mean, surely he has to have compassion and empathy to direct such a place.*

"Ms. Scott, have I lost you?"

"No, I'm with you."

Dr. McKay led Rachel down a long corridor. The clinic was spacious and bright, painted in light pastel colors. Colorful pictures and fresh flowers decorated the walls and tables throughout the clinic.

"How long have you been open?"

"Eighteen months now."

Rachel gave a nervous smile and said, "The décor is quite elegant here."

"Actually, it is quite intimate. You'll see what I mean when we get to the individual rooms."

Rachel wanted to believe him, but her inner voice was telling her things might not be as they seemed.

"Here we are. I told the staff to keep this room empty

for us." Dr. McKay opened the door to a room and directed Rachel inside. The room was about the size of a studio apartment. It was set up like a master suite at the Ritz Plaza and accommodated a full-size bed, modern bedroom furniture, an entertainment center with a thirty-one-inch TV, and a DVD player. Dr. McKay looked like a proud papa whose wife had just given birth to a new baby boy.

"See, I told you. As you can see, we try to provide a home atmosphere. We even encourage our clients to bring special photographs or keepsakes with them. We feel it is important for our clients to be surrounded with whatever gives them feelings of love and peace."

Rachel asked, "How long are your clients usually here?"

"That depends on the circumstances. Usually our clients are here for less than twenty-four hours. However, we believe the atmosphere created for our clients is an essential component of our services."

"Are there usually loved ones here when it—your service—happens?"

Dr. McKay glared at Rachel and said, "That also depends on the circumstance."

"So there are times when the client is alone during the process?"

A nurse entered the room and interrupted.

"Dr. McKay, you have a phone call from Dr. Smith."

Obviously happy for the interruption, Dr. McKay said, "Ms. Scott, please excuse me. I'll be right back, and then we can go to my office."

Rachel breathed a sigh of relief as Dr. McKay exited the room. *What is it?* There was something there, but Rachel

23

couldn't put her finger on it. Rachel began to walk around the room examining, touching, and feeling until emotions began to rise in her.

Tears were beginning to build in her eyes. She stared intently at the bed, and suddenly a memory exploded in her mind. She was looking at a sterile room. She was a child, and her Grandpa James was sitting in a wheelchair. Rachel was walking around the bed toward her grandfather. She looked into his eyes and smiled brightly.

"Grandpa, why do you look so sad?"

Rachel's grandpa looked confused as he answered the young child. "It's okay, Linda. I know you love me."

Rachel giggled. "Linda's my mom, but I'll be Linda today." Rachel reached for her grandfather's neck and embraced him. "Yes, I do love you."

The door opened quickly as Dr. McKay rushed back into the room. Rachel was startled and snapped back to reality.

"Sorry about the interruption. I'd like to finish our tour and then go to my office for your interview."

Rachel took a deep breath. "Yes, thank you."

Rachel and Dr. McKay continued to walk through the corridor until they entered a large, bright room surrounded by windows. The view of the outdoor landscaping was breathtaking.

Inside the room were leather couches and recliner chairs to assist anyone whose purpose was to sit and reflect. An older gentleman, clearly distraught, sat in one of the recliners now. He stared out the window and appeared to be fighting to hold back tears. Rachel could feel the man's pain and desperately wanted to comfort him.

Her attention turned back to Dr. McKay as he said, "This is our Reflection Room. It is for our patients' families. Sometimes loved ones just need to reflect or make peace with the process here."

"I can only imagine. Do you have a psychologist on staff?"

"No. But we have an excellent staff of social workers. In fact, each client is assigned a social worker who meets with the client and loved ones before and after admission."

Rachel recalled a conversation she had had once with a nurse friend. Her friend had been nursing in a hospital for almost thirty years. The friend surmised that social workers over the years were forced to take on responsibilities of nurses and psychologists—basically any responsibilities that involved communication. The nurse described her role as task-orientated. Anything further was left to the social worker. That recollection made Rachel uneasy about Dr. McKay's answer.

"Are the social workers here trained to intervene with distraught families?"

"Oh yes, all staff here are required to take an end-of-life workshop."

Great, Rachel thought sarcastically. "So everything is pretty up-front? I mean, when the clients come here, it is clearly to end their lives, and everyone knows it?" Rachel looked over toward the older man sitting in the chair. Tears now flowed down his cheeks.

Dr. McKay caught the glance. He did not answer Rachel but motioned toward the corridor and said, "Should we continue?"

Rachel followed Dr. McKay until they stopped at a door

with some gold lettering that read, *Dr. Bill McKay, Director*. Dr. McKay took a key from his pocket and unlocked the door. As they entered his office, Rachel couldn't help thinking this office could match any CEO listed in *Fortune* magazine. The decor was unique and expensive.

"Can I offer you anything to drink?"

"No, thank you. I'm fine. This is a nice office."

Dr. McKay caught the understatement and felt compelled to explain the necessity of such a plush environment. "This job can at times be, let's say, *emotional*. There are times I enjoy the escape here."

Rachel jumped into journalist mode. "Can you describe one of your 'emotional' experiences?"

"I'll try, but we must maintain a high level of confidentiality. I can tell you in general there are some families that are confused about the dying process. We do our best to assure them that our process is painless and dignified."

Rachel looked up from her pad, careful not make direct eye contact. "I'd like to hear about the process. Is it similar to the lethal injections given to prisoners on death row?"

Dr. McKay shifted in his chair. He was uncomfortable with the question. "No, no. We use a potassium-based medication. It is really very peaceful."

Rachel quickly wrote a note to check out the process of capital punishment by injection. Somehow she doubted the process was that different. She looked up and remarked, "The concept sounds the same. I mean, last year we had to put our dog to sleep. I was in there with her, and the process was very peaceful."

"I'm not sure we can compare this process to putting your pet down or lethal injections for prisoners."

Rachel was faced with the decision of pushing further and risking Dr. McKay shutting her off, or going in a new direction for more answers. She chose the latter. "We've only been talking about the final process. Perhaps we should start at the beginning. What would drive a person to the decision of entering your clinic?"

"There are many reasons. The main one is the diagnosis of a terminal illness. There is really no hope for healing. The pain is uncontrollable, or they become dependent on others. Our clinic is really an answer to their prayers."

"What kind of terminal illness?"

"Usually it's the kind of illness that leaves a client dependent upon others. Like cancer, ALS, or Alzheimer's."

That peaked Rachel's interest. Her Grandpa James had died of Alzheimer's, and over the years she had stayed educated about the disease. "In the case of an Alzheimer's client, isn't it the caregivers who are deciding that euthanasia is the best solution?"

"Of course, it has to be."

"What if the reason is that the caregiver is tired or too busy to be bothered?"

Dr. McKay answered defensively, "Listen, the horrible truth is that the Alzheimer's clients eventually have no quality of life. They just aren't the same people."

Rachel decided to push. "So is that a determining factor for admission—quality of life?"

"Yes, it's one of them."

"Who determines the quality of the client's life?"

"The clients themselves, if they are able, and of course the family or caregiver."

Rachel dug deeper. "What about the other factors for admission?"

"Well, basically it is a choice to end life with dignity."

"So it's a question of dignity. Dignity in dying when there is no dignity in living."

"Look, it's getting late. Perhaps we could finish this tomorrow. Say, ten o'clock tomorrow morning."

Rachel agreed. She would have preferred to catch a flight home tonight but was more than willing to extend her trip another day to interview Dr. McKay further. Besides, she wanted to backtrack her steps to see if the gentleman in the Reflection Room was still there.

She said her good-byes to Dr. McKay and saw her way out of his office. Rachel had an uneasy feeling about Dr. McKay and his humane efforts toward a dignified death. Rachel's heart was whispering something, and she intended to find out what it was.

There was good reason for Rachel's uneasy feelings. Dr. McKay wasn't necessarily interested in serving humanity. He was driven by one thing: greed. In the early 1980s, when the statistics on geriatric growth circulated, Dr. McKay knew that serving the older population was his future path.

For over a decade Dr. McKay preyed on the older generation's desire to conquer death. He recommended procedures that in the past would have never been considered for that age group. Now it was common practice to perform transplants, open-heart surgeries, and prescribe just about any medication on the market to the aged population.

Dr. McKay had made a nice living over the years with his defying-death philosophy, but this new shift in thinking could make his wealth limitless. He spoke *death with dignity*, *ending the suffering*, or whatever cliché it took to get clients into his clinic.

Rachel made her way back to the Reflection Room. She located the older gentleman right away. He appeared to be almost in a trance-like state now. Rachel walked slowly to his side and sat down on an adjacent chair.

"Hello. My name is Rachel. I couldn't help noticing how deep in thought you look. Are you all right?"

"Hi, I'm Walter Stafford. No, I'm not all right. I think I'm in shock. I feel numb all over."

"I'm so sorry, Walter. What happened? Do you have a loved one here?"

"My Gracie. She's gone now. It was her decision. I should have stopped her. We should have found another way."

"Another way for what, Walter?"

"Another way to take care of her. She just didn't want to die in a nursing home."

Rachel scooted up on her chair to get closer to Walter. "Is that why Gracie came here, because she was going in a nursing home?"

"I couldn't take care of her. We could have hired someone to come into our home for a while. But Gracie didn't want a stranger living in our home, taking care of her. Our children have their own lives. She pretended to be so brave."

A lump formed in Rachel's throat. "I'm sure she was very brave."

Walter was now sobbing. "No, she was desperate. I can see that now. Her eyes were so scared and confused. It is just so surreal. I can't believe yesterday we thought ten thousand dollars was a bargain to remove the burden of Gracie's care. I can't believe we did it."

"Excuse me, Walter. What do you mean, *ten thousand dollars*?"

"That is what the services here cost."

Rachel took a deep breath and paused before speaking. "Walter, how did you find out about this place?"

Walter had retrieved a handkerchief from his pocket and wiped his eyes. "Oh, our family physician, Dr. Kramer. He gave us Dr. McKay's phone number."

Rachel had a thousand questions popping out at her. She looked into Walter's eyes, and her compassion took over. "Is there anything I can do for you, Walter? Can I call someone for you?"

Walter was about to answer when a large women interrupted their conversation. "That won't be necessary. Hello, Walter, I've been trying to get out here to check on you."

"Oh, hi. This is Rachel. I've been telling her I'm not sure we did the right thing."

The women glared at Rachel as if looks could kill. Then she turned her attention back to Walter. "It's difficult to sort out your emotions right now. Remember, we talked about that. Let's go to my office and talk privately."

"Do you work here?" Rachel asked.

"Yes, I'm Walter's social worker. Are you ready, Walter?"

Walter stood to go then stopped and turned toward Rachel. "It was nice to meet you, Rachel. Maybe you should think about this before you do anything."

Rachel stood and gave Walter a quick hug. She whispered, "Take care of yourself, Walter."

As Walter and the social worker walked off together, Rachel looked out the massive window and fought back tears. Her thoughts returned to Grandpa James. She realized that this story would involve more than just reporting on the services provided by Peaceful Transitions.

All of a sudden it was as if the very walls of Peaceful Transitions were crying out to her. Rachel called a cab from her cell phone and decided to wait outside. She couldn't wait to get to her hotel and call home.

Rachel had called downstairs and ordered room service. She was shoveling down her food like someone who had just been rescued from a deserted island. She stopped herself and took a deep breath. She wondered what was disturbing her so much. Was it the uneasy feeling she had gotten with Dr. McKay or Walter's grief?

Rachel decided to write her thoughts down in bullets. She was a visual person, and something about having things outlined on paper helped her synthesize her thoughts. She started listing everything she could remember about the day and realized what was eating at her; the massive payment Walter had paid for Gracie's euthanasia. Her mind started multiplying that figure by the number of possible clients. She resolved to dig further into the financial situation at Peaceful Transitions.

She looked at the clock and opened her cell phone then dialed a familiar number and waited for Kyle to answer.

"Hello."

"Hi, honey, how are you?"

"Great! We just got back from Sarah's dance practice."

Rachel thought she detected a rushed tone in Kyle's voice. She asked, "Is everything okay?"

"Yeah, we're fine. I'm just trying to throw some dinner together."

"I miss you guys."

Kyle paused before he answered. "You really sound, ah, sad."

Actually, Rachel wanted to start crying. But she didn't want to alarm Kyle, so she held back the tears. "I don't know. There's a lot of emotion coming from that clinic. Kyle, I met this man who just had his wife, well . . ."

"Terminated?"

"Kyle, please. It's not like that. The director actually makes it sound like a compassionate, reasonable option for families. But somehow it just *feels* wrong. Walter—the man I met—he felt so guilty. He was questioning the choice he and his wife had made. I'm not sure how a family *can* make choices like that."

"Rachel, you are probably the most objective person I know. What is really going on here?"

"I started thinking about my Grandpa James. You know my grandpa had Alzheimer's and my mom placed him in a nursing home. He always seemed so unhappy in the nursing home. I wonder if things might have been different for our family if Peaceful Transitions had existed back then."

"Listen, honey, the journalist is coming out of you, and you have some questions. Do what you always do. Jump in to find out."

"Right, I hear you. I'll be home tomorrow afternoon. Thanks for listening."

"You're welcome. I love you."

"I love you too. Tell Sarah and Laura I love them too."

"Have a safe trip. Try to get some sleep."

Rachel hung up the phone and thanked God for such a good husband. She knew he would give her the moon if she asked and he could.

Rachel was eager to approach Dr. McKay tomorrow with questions about the numbers of clients serviced at Peaceful Transitions.

Rachel had no trouble getting to sleep. Sometime during the night she started having dreams that caused her to toss and turn. Her Grandpa James was sitting in his wheelchair crying. She was a little girl trying to comfort him. As Rachel abruptly awoke, she looked around to check her surroundings. She looked at the clock and realized it was the middle of the night in her hotel room. She reached for the remote and turned on the television to lull herself back to sleep.

The next morning Rachel walked into Peaceful Transitions and was greeted by the receptionist. "If you would follow me, Dr. McKay has requested that your meeting be held at our outside patio."

Rachel followed the receptionist outside and took a seat at a shaded table.

"Dr. McKay thought you might enjoy the fresh air. He'll be with you soon. Can I get you anything?"

"No, thank you. I'm fine."

As the receptionist walked away, Rachel felt as though she had been purposely kept out of the building. Had the social worker from yesterday said something to Dr. McKay about her conversation with Walter? She was beginning to feel uneasy again. She decided to get right to the point with her questions when the doctor joined her.

"Good morning, Ms. Scott. I trust you slept well last night."

"No. Actually I didn't."

"I'm sorry to hear that. I'm sure you will be happy to return to your own surroundings."

"Yes, well, there's no place like home."

"Then let's get down to business. Where were we in the interview?"

"Dr. McKay, how do your clients pay for their services at Peaceful Transitions?"

"Most payment is private. The state also assists in financing us. We try to make accommodations for anyone who applies for admission."

"How many clients would you say you serve daily?"

Dr. McKay's eyes begin to narrow as he replied, "It varies. We are getting admissions from all over the country right now."

"Well, on average, about how many?"

"On average I'd say ten to fifteen clients daily."

It was all Rachel could do to contain herself. The numbers were more than she had imagined. She stayed on task and asked, "Are the fees approximately the same for each client?"

"Well, like I said, we will work with our clients, but on the average, yes."

"Dr. McKay, are there groups that oppose your services here? I mean, have you received threatening phone calls or letters?"

"Not so much now. There was more protest in the beginning stages. There were church groups that got on Fox and other cable channels claiming we were murderers. But the public understands the right to choice. Things have quieted down now. The point is, we are operating within the law."

"Has the federal government opposed it in any way?"

"A couple of senators. One of them, Senator Green, has a mother with Alzheimer's. He has been on a mission to ban euthanasia. But most of the people in Washington, DC prefer to leave moral issues up to the states."

"What about the American Medical Association? Do they support legalized euthanasia?"

"The AMA isn't ready to support our services. But there are a large growing number of physicians who support a patient's right to die with dignity."

Rachel closed her notepad as she said, "Thank you, Dr. McKay. I believe that is all the information I need for now. Could I call with any follow-up questions that might come up?"

"Yes, of course, Ms. Scott. It has been a pleasure to meet you."

"Likewise. I'll show myself out." Rachel wasn't sincere about it being a pleasure to meet with Dr. McKay, but she doubted he was sincere either. The truth was, they distrusted each other, and both with good reason.

Rachel called a cab then called Kyle's cell phone. She knew he was in classes but wanted to leave him a message that she was on her way home and stopping by her office for a while. She took one last look at Peaceful Transitions as she climbed into her cab and started home.

4

Rachel entered the building of *Situational Life* Magazine. She was anxious to get on her computer and start making an outline of today's interview. She also wanted to find out more about Dr. McKay and the financial history at Peaceful Transitions. She stepped off the elevator to find Rusty standing there to greet her. "Hi, Rusty, how's it going?"

"Great!" He handed her the latest copy of their magazine. "Good story on long-term care. I think it will open some eyes. How was the interview in Oregon?"

"There's more to it than I had thought. I might need some time to sort it out."

"I can tell your wheels are spinning. Do you want to talk about it?"

"Yeah, I guess so. Let me put my things down, and I'll join you in your office."

Rachel took some time at her desk to put things in their proper places. She had been told that she was organized to a fault. She knew it didn't matter what others thought. She couldn't function any other way.

As Rachel sat down across from Rusty at his desk, he said, "You look beat. Maybe you should go home and take a nap."

"No, I'm fine. I just feel like I need to get some answers before I start this story."

"What kind of answers?"

"Dr. McKay talks about his clinic as if it's the saving grace to the dying. Maybe it is, but my gut tells me there's more to it."

In all the years Rusty had known Rachel, her gut had told her amazing things. He was listening intently as he asked, "What kinds of things is your gut telling you?"

"Things like where one hundred thousand dollars a day is going. I met a man named Walter. His wife was a client at the clinic. He told me he paid ten thousand dollars for the services. Dr. McKay said they have ten or more clients daily. Plus, the state supplements the clinic for its services. That's an awful lot of money."

"Okay, go ahead and research or do what you need to do. I know a minister who does a lot of grief counseling. The local hospitals call on him. His name is Peter Wade. Here's his phone number. I think he might be a good contact for you."

"Thanks. I'll give him a call."

Rachel stopped surfing the Internet and called Peter Wade. "Hello, this is Rachel Scott from *Situational Life* Magazine. I'd like to speak to Peter Wade please."

"Yes, just a minute please."

"Hello, this is Peter Wade speaking."

"Hello, this is Rachel Scott from *Situational Life* Magazine."

"Hi, Rachel, how are you?"

Peter's voice was pleasant and sincere. Rachel could already sense the comfort he must give to hurting people. "I'm doing fine. My boss, Rusty Richlin, gave me your phone number. I'm writing a story about some end-of-life issues and would like to speak with you if possible."

"Sure, when would you like to meet?"

"How about tomorrow morning?"

"That would be great. Are you familiar with Phoenix Community Church on San Vincente Street?"

"Yes. Thank you, Pastor Wade, I'll see you tomorrow."

Rachel looked at the clock on her desk and grabbed the phone again. She dialed her home, and Stacy answered, "Hello, Scott residence."

"Hi, Stacy. It's Rachel. Is Sarah getting ready for her recital?"

"Yes, I'm doing her hair now."

"I really appreciate your help. Did you manage to get your homework done?"

"Yes, I finished most of it at school."

"Thanks, Stacy. I'll be there to pick the girls up soon."

Rachel shut down her computer and packed her notepad and pens into her leather bag. She reflected on her upcoming meeting with Peter Wade and hoped he could answer some of the nagging questions she had about quality of life.

Rachel picked up Sarah and Laura in plenty of time to grab Carl's Jr on the way. She and Laura were sitting in the audience while Sarah was backstage with the other performers.

Kyle sat down in the seat Rachel had been saving for him. "Hi, stranger, I missed you."

Rachel leaned over and gave Kyle a quick kiss. "I missed you too. I can't believe Sarah's recital is finally here. She's so excited."

Laura shook Rachel's arm and asked, "Mama, is your story a happy story?"

Rachel paused. "No, honey, it's not so happy."

"Why? We wanted a happy story."

"I'm sorry, honey, but all stories can't be happy."

Kyle took Rachel's hand and said, "You really look tired."

"I admit I'm looking forward to bed."

Kyle squeezed her hand. "That makes two of us."

The recital began as the lights dimmed. Sarah danced across the stage with her peers. She spotted her family, and they exchanged smiles.

5

The Meadowbrook Country Club was exclusive to the most elite in Portland, Oregon. Two men entered the men's locker room with tennis rackets in hand. Dr. McKay had just finished playing a game of tennis with Dr. Tom Kramer. Neither one of them could play much above a beginning level, but they loved walking around appearing professional.

Dr. McKay turned toward Dr. Kramer and whispered, "I'm not comfortable with the Rachel Scott interview."

"Then why did you give it?"

"You know—for the exposure, free marketing. Last meeting the board mentioned expanding."

"Yeah, when the time is right. We still have Senator

Green out there preaching against us. I think you jumped the gun, buddy!"

"Well, I can't change that now. I'm just saying we better make some calls to find out where the story's headed."

"I'll take care of it. Meanwhile, you better keep your mouth shut."

Rachel entered Phoenix Community Church. The church was a newer building. It was a nondenominational congregation. Rachel liked the concept and had considered visiting sometime. She spotted a middle-aged man wearing jeans and a sweater coming toward her.

"Hi, you must be Rachel." Peter was smiling.

"Yes, I'm Rachel. You must be, ah, Pastor Wade or Pastor Peter?"

Peter laughed loudly. "No, just Peter is fine."

"Sorry, I wasn't sure about the appropriate terminology these days."

"No apology necessary. So, Rachel, you said on the phone you were writing a story on end-of-life issues."

"Yes, I am. In fact, I was in Oregon yesterday at Peaceful Transitions. Are you familiar with the clinic?"

"As a matter of fact, I am. The truth is that I'm not an advocate for euthanasia or the clinic."

Rachel was taken aback by Peter's frankness. It seemed to be a rare trait these days. Rachel found that most people seemed to straddle the fence and had a hard time coming out and saying what they really meant. This was particularly true when she interviewed people. She attributed this to her being a journalist and people trying to be careful with their words because they suspected she would twist them. Peter led Rachel to his office, and she couldn't help noticing the modest décor compared to Dr. McKay's.

Rachel said, "I have to admit I'm a bit confused about the concept of euthanasia."

"You mean the concept of death with dignity."

"Yes, and also knowing when the client's quality of life is no longer worth preserving."

"Yeah, society in general is confused. I personally feel we got ourselves into trouble with the end-of-life terminology. When we started introducing advanced directives and instruction for how clients wanted to live out the ends of their lives, it became confusing. Too many people confused that with euthanasia. We really should have called it *rest-of-life* issues."

"That does sound different. I mean, it just sounds more hopeful."

"Exactly; you see, the concept was to give clients the freedom to plan how they wanted to live out the rest of their days. With or without medication, life support, tube feedings, things like that. It even extends emotionally and spiritually. In other words, when clients are told they have a terminal illness, they can plan the rest of their lives as they see fit. In some cases that includes eternal life."

"What kind of organization would assist families with *rest-of-life* issues?"

"The Hospice Foundation is really good at taking care of the terminally ill. They address everything from physical to spiritual issues."

"It sounds like hospice supports a more natural way of dying as opposed to intentionally ending life. I never really thought about the difference."

Peter nodded. "You're not alone, Rachel. But there is a difference between choosing to die naturally or choosing lethal injection."

"What about pain and suffering? What if it gets too much for the client to handle?"

"That's a good question. With the medication available today, we can pretty much control most pain. The suffering is another matter. That's usually emotional and the experience can be the client's or caregiver's."

"Perhaps it is those suffering clients who need a place like Peaceful Transitions."

"Unfortunately, they're the ones who get exploited by Peaceful Transitions. They are confused, tired, desperate, or just angry. Instead of coming to terms with the illness, they want to control the illness."

Something clicked for Rachel, and she said, "And they believe they have no quality of life. Dying is the most dignified thing to do for everyone involved."

"That's right. The natural dying process is too overwhelming. The fact is, it takes a lot of courage for the client and loved ones to embrace the dying process. The sad part is, society doesn't embrace dying as a brave thing. But I've seen many families turn around and find peace with hospice support."

Rachel looked over her notes. "What about those who are facing skilled nursing admission? When the thought of being in a nursing home is too much for them?"

Peter sighed. "Yeah, that's where the country is failing

our elders. If you want to talk about lack of dignity, then you should explore the permanent institutions where we place our elders."

"I thought those places were regulated by the state. Don't they have to meet certain standards?"

"The standards have improved over the past twenty years, especially in relation to medications, restraints, and abuse. But there is a real lack of dementia knowledge out there. Staff don't understand the disease process or the behaviors associated with the cognitive diseases, and they definitely don't understand how to communicate with dementia clients."

"My mother had a really hard time communicating with my grandpa. He was in a nursing home. Are there any quality nursing homes that you know of?"

"As a matter of fact, I just met a lady named Catherine Perez. She recently opened up her own Alzheimer's facility. She specializes in communication techniques. You might think about visiting." Peter turned his Rolodex and found Catherine's phone number. "Here's her phone number if you'd like to call her. If you do decide to visit her, give me a call. I'd love to take a look myself."

"I'll set up an appointment with Catherine and let you know. Why do you think the government hasn't intervened with euthanasia practices?"

Peter leaned back in his chair and put his hands behind his head. Rachel felt comfortable with Peter. She could feel his passion for people.

Peter responded thoughtfully, "A couple of reasons. One, the people of this nation have made it loud and clear how they feel about the government intervening with personal-choice issues. Look at abortion and same-sex marriage. However, more and more our federal government is mandating ethical and moral behavior for our society. Secondly, with the baby boomers, quite frankly, the nation is in a crisis how to care for them. It's sad, but I have heard that some politicians even think euthanasia is a blessing because it could take some of the pressure off the budget."

"Now that sounds rather desperate. Goodness, I hope that's not true."

"I believe it is true, Rachel; desperate and true."

Rachel paused as she looked over her notes, "Well, thanks, Peter. You've given me some things to think about. I have a feeling this story isn't going to be as simple as informing the public about the services of Peaceful Transitions."

"It's been my pleasure. Bless you for seeking the truth, and please don't forget about Catherine."

Rachel was sitting in her living room with a full glass of wine. She had been staring into space for a while, deep in thought. She wondered how many people like her had given little or no thought to the dying process. If she had her way, she would die instantly in an accident or in the middle of the night, but if she were faced with an actual process, would she be able to die with grace? There was so much involved, and it affected everyone close to you. Rachel looked down at her glass and took a sip.

Kyle walked into the room and sat down next to Rachel. He wrapped his arms around her and gave her a kiss as they embraced. Kyle whispered, "Hey you, a penny for your thoughts."

"Hi, honey, I'm thinking about someone I met today. I talked to a minister who specializes in grief counseling. I'm trying to digest his perspective."

"Sounds like he probably has a lot of personal experience."

"Yes, he does. He seems very sure in what he knows. He isn't a fan of euthanasia."

Kyle half-chuckled and said, "I wouldn't imagine he would be. He is a minister. It would be kind of hard to preach, 'Thou shalt not kill (except if it's the right choice for you or your family).'"

"I'm shocked, Kyle. I had no idea you felt this way about euthanasia."

"I didn't say I did."

"Well, most churches today don't really get involved with moral issues that involve ending life; for example, abortion and capital punishment."

Kyle took a sip of Rachel's wine and looked intently at her. "So, what are you thinking?"

Rachel breathed in deeply and let it out. "I'm thinking I understand how families could feel driven toward euthanasia. But I'm wondering if the people who run the clinic are likewise driven. In other words, could someone like Dr. McKay have other motives for supporting euthanasia? And I'm uncomfortable with the way society is just accepting this."

"Maybe it's the money. That could be the motive for

starting the clinic. It's easy for some people to monopolize from a subtle deceit when they are profiting from it."

"That's true. Peter, the minister I met with today, said that maybe the government is purposely turning its head because of the crisis of the baby boomers."

"Well, that wouldn't surprise me one bit."

"Yes, but if that's true, the feds' complacency breeds perfect ground for parasites to feed on hurting people."

"Well, it wouldn't be the first time. Look at the situation of our economy. Turning heads while getting their backs scratched is what feds do best; or at least the majority of them."

"I know. Tomorrow I'll look into the financial history of the clinic. I'm exhausted. I'm going to hit the sack." Rachel gave Kyle a long kiss. "I'll see you upstairs."

Rachel decided to take a soak in the tub before bed. As she sat with her head resting on the edge of the tub, she let her mind wander. She starting thinking about her childhood and growing up in Carmel, California. Her memories were lonely ones. She was an only child, and both her parents had been active in their community. Her father was a workaholic, and her mother was busy trying to keep up with the Joneses. Actually, Rachel had never been planned; her mother became pregnant while in her forties.

The saving grace in Rachel's childhood had been her maternal grandfather, Grandpa James. Grandpa James had become afflicted with Alzheimer's disease shortly after the death of his wife. Rachel was only seven when he came to live with her family. He showered her with affection, and she relished the attention. Rachel smiled at the memories until she remembered the day Grandpa James had left their home for good.

Rachel's memory went to a time in her childhood when she stood staring through her living room window, watching her mother help Grandpa James into the car. It was a sad memory, for somehow, even in a child's mind, she knew Grandpa James would never return.

That day Grandpa James was admitted into Brunridge Convalescent Home, and even though Rachel was allowed to visit him there, things were forever different.

Rachel drifted asleep on her side and began to dream about Grandpa James. They were at her favorite park in Carmel. Grandpa James was pushing Rachel on the swing. They were both laughing freely.

The dream changed to the both of them sitting on a park bench and eating ice cream. Rachel looked into her grandfather's eyes and said, "Grandpa, where did you used to work?"

Grandpa James responded, "I can't remember. I've been having some trouble with my memory lately."

"Mom gets really mad when you forget."

Grandpa James smiled gently. "I know, Rachel. But she's not really mad at me. She's afraid of what's happening to me."

"I'm not afraid, Grandpa James. I'll never get mad at you."

Grandpa James couldn't hold back the tears. "I know, my little sweetness. You are a very special girl, Rachel."

Rachel's dreams turned dark. She began to toss and turn in bed. She saw a strange room with a bed in the middle of it. As the bed got closer, she saw her Grandpa James lying in the bed with an IV in his arm. Rachel heard loud echoes of Dr. McKay's voice.

"It's time, James. It's time, James. It's time, James."

Rachel awoke suddenly and looked over to Kyle. He was sound asleep. Rachel lay on her back and stared at the ceiling for what seemed like eternity.

It was midafternoon, and Rachel had been trying to work on her story. The restless night before had left her unable to focus. She was having conflicting feelings about end-of-life, quality-of-life issues.

Rachel had a sudden urge to see Kyle. She jumped up from her desk, grabbed her suit jacket, and exited the office.

Rachel entered the history wing of Phoenix Community College. She knew what she needed to do but needed Kyle's support. Rachel walked down the short hallway and peeked into Kyle's classroom. Kyle stood in front of his class waving a pencil as he talked about World War I. She loved watching

Kyle teach. She knew his students loved his quick wit and true passion for history.

Rachel waited briefly as Kyle ended his class. Kyle spotted her as he dismissed his class, and her dodged her way through the students to reach him.

Kyle smiled as he said, "Well, to what do I owe this pleasure?"

"Hi, honey. Do you have a minute?"

"Yeah, but let's take a walk. I need a break from the classroom. You were pretty restless last night."

Rachel looked down. "I know. Listen, I'm thinking about visiting my mother. Well, really I'd like to visit Grandpa James's grave."

"Okay, do you need to talk to him or need something from him?"

Rachel smiled at Kyle's response. Kyle had to know this was out of character for her. "Something like that. I need to talk to my mom too."

"What about?"

"I feel like something bad happened with Grandpa James. I believe he might have felt abandoned by Mom."

"Well, what if he did? Is your mom going to tell you that?"

Rachel hadn't expected resistance from Kyle. She wasn't exactly sure why she felt so driven to go home. "She might. I don't know. I just feel as though this is important."

Kyle took her hand in his and sweetly said, "Okay, but I'd like to wait until this weekend so the girls and I can drive you. I'll get a sub for my class Monday."

Rachel felt as though a weight had been lifted off her

shoulder. "I'd really like that. I called Mom this afternoon, and I know she'll be home."

"Good. Hopefully you'll be able to sleep better after our trip."

"And have a clear direction on my story. Hey, I better let you go." Rachel kissed Kyle on the lips longer than she normally would at his work. "Thank you, Kyle."

"Anything for you," Kyle said as he held his hand over his heart.

The gold plaque was engraved with Senator O'Connor's name and title. She was sitting at her desk, and her aide, Richard Kemp, stood across from her. Richard was filing through Senator O'Connor's messages. "Did you return Dr. Kramer's call? It sounded urgent."

The Senator answered curtly, "Yes, I did, Richard. And quite frankly, I'm getting disgusted with reporters and fellow colleagues of mine trying to stick their noses into my state's business."

Richard's eyebrow lifted. "You're referring to the Senate hearing?"

"You know darn well that's what I'm referring to. It's ridiculous the way these people won't let go. Our states can't continue to carry the burden for Medicare-age people. God knows our federal government can't do the job. If they want to end it early, I say let them."

"Are you still going to testify to the commission?"

"I don't see where I have a choice. I have to testify."

"Maybe it's more than just the moral and ethical implications. Maybe they know Dr. Kramer is your distant—or should I say, *kissing*—cousin."

Senator O'Connor stood up. "This conversation is over, Richard. You know too much. Remember, what you know *can* hurt you."

Richard said half-sarcastically, "I know nothing, I see nothing, and I do nothing."

"Fine, keep it that way." Senator O'Connor grabbed her briefcase and rushed out the door.

As Rachel helped Kyle pack their Ford Explorer, she stopped to absorb the warmth of a perfect spring day. She loved the Phoenix weather. That reminded her to check for sweatshirts.

Carmel, California, was located on the Pacific Ocean and was as different as night from day compared to Phoenix. The gloomy fog that could consume the Carmel air, along with the ocean breeze, were capable of chilling a person to the bone. Unfortunately the unpredictable weather in Carmel extended right through the summer months. Her childhood home hadn't required air conditioning, and her mother slept with an electric blanket every night. Rachel thought, *It sure isn't Baywatch!*

"Girls, let's get going. We have a long trip ahead."

Kyle shoved the last of the suitcases and closed the hatch. "Mom's right. Let's get a move on."

The girls jumped into the SUV. They immediately started arranging the pillows and blankets in the backseat. Kyle and Rachel fastened their seatbelts as they pulled away from their house. Rachel looked out the window and wondered what answers awaited her in Carmel. She closed her eyes and soon drifted into a deep sleep.

Kyle steered the Explorer up a winding, steep hill in Carmel. The trip had been uneventful with Rachel and the girls sleeping a majority of the way. Rachel reached to the backseat and gently woke the girls. "Hi, you sleepy-heads. We're at Grandma Linda's."

Sarah stretched as she looked out the window in silence.

Laura squealed, "Yay! Mom, when can we go to the beach?"

"We'll see. But remember, the water is probably too cold for swimming."

Sarah asked quietly, "Can we play in the sand or look for seashells?"

"Of course we can, honey."

Kyle pulled into Linda's driveway, which led to a large, beautifully maintained home. Linda was waiting at the doorway as if she knew the exact moment her family would arrive. Waving, Linda yelled, "Hi, all of you. Come give Grandma a big hug."

Laura was the first to embrace her grandmother. Linda said, "Laura, tell your mother she should bring you more often."

Rachel and Kyle exchanged a look, and Rachel responded, "Mom, you know we come when we can."

"Well, that's just not good enough. I miss my granddaughters."

Kyle began unloading suitcases. "Sorry, Linda. You know you're always welcome to visit us. We'd buy you a plane ticket any time you like."

Linda quickly changed the subject. She had never

accepted Rachel's decision to make her home away from Carmel. Because of those feelings, Rachel and Kyle suspected, her visits were few and far between. "Come on, let's get inside. I have plenty of things in the fridge for lunch. I'm sure you're hungry."

Laura, still holding on to Linda's hand, asked, "Do you have peanut butter?"

"Yes, I do. And I believe jelly also."

As Rachel began helping Kyle with the suitcases, he gave her a kiss on the cheek. "Go on in and help your mom with lunch. I'll take care of unloading the car."

"Thanks."

Lunch was quiet; most of the conversation revolved around Sarah and Laura's school activities. Rachel and Linda moved in unison as they cleaned the kitchen. Rachel felt uncomfortable starting a conversation with Linda about her reasons for coming.

She took a deep breath as she spoke. "Mom, Kyle and I are going to visit Grandpa's grave this afternoon. You can go with us if you want, but I was hoping to leave the girls with you."

"Why do you want to visit Grandpa's grave? You haven't visited his grave in years."

"I know. But I've been having these dreams about him lately, and I'd like to go."

"My goodness, Rachel; you must be in early menopause."

"No, Mom, it's not my hormones. I really don't want to talk about it right now. But I do want to talk later."

"All right. Of course I'd be happy to watch the girls, but I don't understand." Linda raised her voice. "I did the best I could with your grandfather."

"I really want to believe that, Mom."

The fog had already rolled into Carmel. Rachel's father had called it "the gloom of doom." Rachel pulled her sweatshirt on as the cold Pacific breeze engulfed her body.

Kyle wrapped his arms around her as they approached Grandpa James's gravesite. "You're shaking."

Rachel pulled away from Kyle and said, "Do you mind waiting for me here? I'd like to be alone a few minutes."

"No problem. I'll be right here."

Rachel moved closer to Grandpa James's headstone. She kneeled down and placed a bouquet of flowers by the headstone. "Hi, Grandpa, it's Rachel. I'm sorry I haven't been here for so long. I've really missed you."

Rachel closed her eyes and began to remember a time when she was a child and holding her grandpa's hand. They were smiling at one another as they walked toward her school.

Rachel opened her eyes and stared at the headstone. "Oh, Grandpa, I loved you so much. At times yours was the only love I felt. I wish I could have helped you."

Tears began to flow down Rachel's cheeks.

She closed her eyes again, and more memories began to flow. She was a child sitting on the stairway while her parents talked. She could hear her mother talking to her father.

Linda was upset and spoke in a loud voice. "Honestly, John, I wish Dad would just die. He has no quality of life left. He doesn't even know who I am. He just sits there in his chair and stares out the window or cries. We'll all be better off when he's gone."

"For goodness' sake, Linda, you sound so darn heartless."

"Heartless, my foot. Dad has no dignity left."

Rachel remembered herself running up the stairs. She ran to her room crying and threw herself on her bed. She was a hurt, confused child and began to talk to herself. "What happened to Grandpa's dignity? Where did it go? I wish it would come back. I don't want him to die."

Rachel opened her eyes and the memory was gone. She stared at her grandpa's grave as tears flowed. Kyle walked up and put his arm around Rachel's shoulder.

"Are you all right, Rachel?"

"Yes, it's just that he must have been so lonely at the end."

"That's not your fault, and you can't change the past. But maybe you could help someone else."

"What do you mean?"

"Well, if you were the one making decisions for your grandpa, what would you have done differently?"

Rachel paused to reflect on Kyle's question then answered, "I'm not sure. Maybe I would have kept him home longer. On some level, I think I've been angry with Mom for putting Grandpa in a nursing home. I think maybe I should tell Mom how I feel."

"I'm not sure that's a good idea. Your mom seems like she has a lot of guilt."

"Maybe so, but don't I owe it to Grandpa?"

Kyle gently lifted Rachel into his arms. "Fair enough.

Then let's go. Honey, I know this is difficult, but I'm really proud of you."

"Thank you, Kyle. I love you so much."

The drive back to Linda's house was silent for Kyle and Rachel. Rachel stared out the car window as they traveled the winding roads of Carmel.

Rachel understood her unresolved feelings about what had happened to Grandpa James. For all these years, she had believed her mom had wanted her grandpa dead just because he was sick. Rachel didn't know what dignity was then, but she gathered that it must be devastating to lose it.

Now Rachel realized that it *was* a question of dignity. But whose? Grandpa James's or Linda's?

Rachel's eyes were still red as she and Kyle walked into Linda's house. She had cried most of the ride home. Kyle quickly gathered Sarah and Laura and took them upstairs to play. Rachel and Linda were alone in the living room.

Linda asked, "Would you like something to drink?"

"Yes, some hot tea would be great."

Rachel sat down on the leather couch and watched her mom exit the room. Rachel looked across the room to the fireplace at a picture of herself and her mom on the mantel. Rachel was concentrating on the picture as Linda entered the living room carrying a tray.

"Thank you, Mom. I'm still chilled to the bone."

"You're used to that hot weather in Arizona. How did things go at the cemetery?"

Rachel's eyes met Linda's. "It was nice to spend some time with Grandpa. I remembered how much I loved him."

"Yes, you were both crazy about each other. I had to take care of the both of you. On top of that, you can add your dad."

"That sounds as though it was quite a burden."

Linda put her teacup down on the coffee table. "It was hard. You don't know what it was like."

Rachel could tell that her mom was getting defensive. "No, Mom, I don't. I imagine you must have felt scared, overwhelmed, and even resentful."

"I just did what I had to do. You just move on."

"When I was at Grandpa's grave I remembered you telling Dad that Grandpa had no dignity. That you wished he would just die."

"Well, I don't recall saying that, but it was a blessing when he died."

"I understand that, but what I'm asking is why you felt Grandpa had no dignity left."

"He didn't even know his own name. He had lost his identity. He couldn't dress himself. He ate like a little child. He just stared into space. He wore diapers. It was just awful."

Rachel took a deep breath and asked, "If you had had a choice to end his life before he died naturally, would you have?"

"What kind of question is that?"

"I mean, if euthanasia had been legal then, would you have considered it?"

"I would have gladly considered it, but your father would have never allowed it."

"Yes, Dad was a very compassionate man."

"Well, it wasn't *his* father. He didn't have a clue what I was going through."

"Mom, please! I know how much you miss Dad, and you shouldn't talk about him like that."

Linda's emotions were shaken. She quivered as she spoke. "Of course I miss him. But I tell you, I'm glad he was taken by a heart attack instead of suffering with a long illness."

"You mean as Grandpa did."

"Believe me, your dad wouldn't have wanted to suffer like that."

"No, but I don't think it would have diminished his dignity or quality of life. I don't believe it did Grandpa's either."

"All I know is, it really hurts to see someone you love in that condition."

"Yes, but don't we owe it to them to make that time as dignified as possible? Don't we have a certain responsibility to deal with it?"

"You haven't experienced it, Rachel. You shouldn't judge me."

"I'm not judging. I'm just saying that if you're ever in that situation I will make sure you maintain the highest quality of life. I promise I will stay connected to your spirit."

Tears seeped out of Linda's eyes. "I know you will. That part of you came from your father. For the record, there are times I do regret my last months with your grandpa. But I still believe I did all I could at the time."

Rachel hugged her mom. "I love you, Mom, but I'm not sure I agree."

The next morning was quiet as Kyle finished packing their SUV. Sarah and Laura had already settled in their seats. Sarah was planning a long nap snuggled against her pillow. Laura had begun a drawing of Grandma Linda's house on her Etch A Sketch.

Linda put her arm around Rachel's waist and said, "It was great to see you. I really wish I could see the girls more often."

Kyle, anxious to start the trip, abruptly answered, "As I said, Linda, you're welcome any time."

Rachel agreed. "Mom, it would be easier for you to come see us. You could fly in a couple of hours."

"I know. It's just I have my bridge on Wednesdays. Oh, you know how hard it is."

"Yes, I do. Goodbye, Mom. I love you."

"I love you too. See you soon."

Rachel fell asleep forty-five minutes into the drive back to Phoenix. Her exhaustion overtook her as she slept for the next two hours.

Kyle pulled into a Carl's Jr and announced a bathroom stop.

Kyle asked Rachel, "Is this all right for lunch?"

"Yeah, sure. I can't believe how out of it I am."

"I can. You're emotionally drained."

"I am, but somehow I feel more equipped to research my story. Girls, let's visit the ladies' room before we order lunch."

Once back in the car, Rachel looked at her husband and smiled. "Thank you again, Kyle, for your support. I would have never done this on my own."

"I know, honey. You're going to write a great story for Rusty."

7

Rachel was glad to get back to work the next day. She placed a call to Tim Duncan, who was a private investigator for the magazine.

"Hi, Tim, this is Rachel."

"Well, to what do I owe this honor?"

"What do you mean, *this honor*?"

Tim laughed and said, "I haven't heard from you in a while, and quite frankly, I miss you like heck!"

"Yeah, yeah, I miss you too, Tim. Listen, I need a favor. I'm looking into a clinic named Peaceful Transitions. I need all the information you can dig up on the director, Dr. Bill McKay, and the board of directors."

"Isn't that the legalized euthanasia clinic in Oregon?"

"That's right. I think there are some questionable things going on there. And I have a bad feeling about Dr. McKay."

"I'll get right on it. You know I love bringing powerful men to their knees!"

"Yes, I know you do. Thank you, and call me as soon as you get anything."

"Will do."

"Bye, Tim."

Rachel looked at her watch and realized she had worked through lunch. She decided to walk over to Quizno's for a quick salad. When she had settled at an outside table, her cell phone rang.

"Hello? Oh, hi, Peter. How are you?"

Peter Wade said, "Fine, thank you. I was wondering if you had any time this afternoon. I'm going to tour New Perceptions and thought you might like to tag along."

Rachel looked at her watch, "Yeah, I'd love to. Are you headed over soon?"

"In about an hour. Would you like me to pick you up?"

"No, I'll meet you there. Thanks, Peter."

Rachel pulled into the New Perceptions parking lot and parked. She was impressed with the landscaping. The colored flowers were bright and welcoming. As Rachel approached the entrance, she noticed a sign to the right of the entryway. The sign read, *This home defines dignity. Will the disease process define our patients' dignity or the environment we create for them?* Rachel reflected on the quote and entered the facility. Peter was standing in the front lobby and spotted her immediately.

"I'm really glad you could join me. The receptionist said Catherine's in her office around the corner. She's expecting us."

The office was modest in size, very organized, and brightly decorated. The furniture appeared to be Ashley décor. Rachel couldn't help comparing it again to Dr. McKay's.

Catherine looked up from her desk and flashed a friendly smile. She stood. "Hi, I'm Catherine. You must be Rachel and Peter. Please sit down."

The three extended greetings as Rachel and Peter sat down. Peter began, "Thank you for this time, Catherine. I've been really anxious to see your place."

Rachel said, "Yes, and I'd love to ask you a few questions if you have the time."

"I'd be happy to discuss anything you would like. I just read your story on long-term care. It was well researched and very insightful."

"Thank you. I learned a lot writing that story. I'm learning a lot with this new one also."

"Peter said you are writing something on euthanasia."

Rachel leaned toward Catherine. "That's right. Actually, the assignment is about a clinic called Peaceful Transitions."

Peter said, "Rachel visited the clinic last week. She met with the director, Dr. McKay."

"Well, I've personally never met Dr. McKay and didn't have the heart to visit the clinic at their open house, but I do know what they practice there."

Rachel could tell she was talking to an expert. She fully intended to pick Catherine's brain. "I'm trying to get an angle on the motives for euthanasia, not only for the general public, but also for those who established the clinic."

Peter asked, "What's to say a caregiver wouldn't use the service because he's waiting to inherit a family fortune?"

"The truth is, the motives for euthanasia are limitless. Sometimes the caregivers themselves don't even know their true motives. They just focus on the disease process instead of trying to connect with the client's spirit."

Rachel asked, "Catherine, do you mind if I take some notes and maybe ask a few more questions before you show us around?"

"I don't mind if Peter doesn't."

"No, I'm very interested in Rachel's research."

"Thank you both. This story is important to me, and I believe it will put a new perspective on *rest-of-life* issues." Peter flashed a big smile. "Catherine, how long has New Perceptions been open?"

"Six months now."

"Is this non-profit or for-profit?"

"It's non-profit. We have a board that oversees things, and donations help run the facility."

"Peter mentioned you practice validation techniques. Can you explain what that is?"

"Yes, it's very basic. First of all, I believe that communication is the foundation of all care. With Alzheimer's disease the client's perception of reality is many times altered. The cognitive changes cannot be healed. So we validate our client's new perception and communicate on that level."

"So instead of trying to alter the clients' perceptions to ours, you work with their perceptions."

"That's pretty much it. In fact, to go a step further, I believe validation is an important technique with any terminal illness. Terminal clients need to have their pain, suffering, fears—everything associated with the dying process—validated."

"Do you believe society is failing to meet those validation needs?"

"In a very big way. Imagine if physicians would tell their patients from day one that they will believe them and address every fear, pain, or suffering. Believe me, clients would face their illnesses with new levels of comfort."

"It sounds as though you know what you're talking about."

"Well, I'd like to give you a tour so you can see for yourself."

"I can't wait, but first a couple more questions."

"Fire away."

"How do the clients or residents pay to live here?"

"I expected that question after your long-term article. Approximately half of our residents have long-term insurance that covers most of their stay. We have ten Medi-Cal beds. The rest is private pay. The cost is about $4,200 monthly. We are able to help on a sliding scale basis because of our non-profit status and donations."

Peter said, "Sometimes I don't know how our seniors make it financially."

"Well, the truth is, only about 10 percent of our elderly population is institutionalized. The other 90 percent are still out in our communities."

Peter's jaw dropped. "You're kidding! I didn't know that. No wonder there's so much despair."

"That's right. There is a high rate of depression among caregivers. If our skilled facilities weren't so bleak, it would help caregivers and clients come to terms with being placed. It's just that right now, most families would do anything to avoid placement."

Rachel had been furiously writing and looked up. "Yes, which is what happened to a man I met at Peaceful Transitions."

Peter sighed and said, "I'm glad I'm able to hear this. I can see I have more work to do in the communities. It would be nice if euthanasia wasn't an option."

Catherine smiled at Peter. "I admire you, Peter, but something really needs to be done at a higher level. Hopefully the Senate hearing investigation into legalized euthanasia will open some eyes. Senator Green has worked so diligently to put the hearing in motion."

Rachel said, "Do you know Senator Green? Dr. McKay mentioned he protested the clinic when it first opened."

"Yes, I know Senator Green quite well. I'll give you his contact number if you'd like to call him."

"I would like that very much. Just one more question. The sign out front—could you explain what it means?"

"Oh yes, my motto. That's what New Perceptions is all about. The staff is trained how to adapt the environment to bring about a safe and dignified place for the residents. Adapting the external environment is easy, but adapting the internal environment is a constant challenge."

"Well, I have to admit I'm lost."

"I'm sorry. The external environment would include the

furniture, railings, music, and even clothing. I'll show you as we tour. The internal is mostly communication, and as you'll see, the external and internal go hand in hand."

Peter said, "Wow! It sounds pretty impressive."

Catherine looked proud. "Thanks, Peter. The key is communication. The staff here know they have to communicate on a level that is beyond reasoning. It is definitely a specialized skill."

Rachel was sure she picked up on a mutual attraction between Peter and Catherine. She found herself thinking of the first time she had met Kyle and smiled for the two in the room with her.

"Is it expensive to obtain the training for this?" Rachel asked.

"Not really. We teach onsite. It does take a special person, though. The Alzheimer's residents react to the caregivers' behavior. In other words, they mirror our emotions. So if someone tends to be fearful or, let's say, pushy, many times they will react accordingly."

Peter asked, "Is that where behavioral problems come from?"

"Yes, usually it derives from some kind of internal stress. Our staff tries to prevent that stress by utilizing communication techniques. Sometimes internal stress occurs anyway. Then other techniques, such as distraction, can be helpful."

"Do you use medication?"

"There are times when medication can complement communication techniques. But we never, ever use medication as a substitute for communication techniques. Let me show you firsthand what we do here. Are you finished, Rachel?"

"Yes, thank you. I can't wait."

Rachel, Peter, and Catherine began their tour walking

down a short hallway. They entered a large, round room sur-rounded by windows. There was a nursing station located at the back of the room. The nursing station was built with a large window that opened into the room. The room con-tained chairs and tables, a chalkboard, games, recreation equipment, and a grand piano. It was very organized with shelves and cupboards throughout.

In the center of the room were chairs arranged in a large circle. Twenty residents were sitting in the chairs. An older gentleman played the piano while the residents sang "Will You Come Home, Bill Bailey?." The energy was high and the mood happy. The first thing that caught Rachel's atten-tion was how well-groomed the residents appeared. To the left of the room was a sliding glass door that led to an outside garden. There were several residents with a staff member arranging various potted plants.

Catherine motioned toward the residents. "This is our activity room. Our residents are in this room a lot during the day. We have two or three staff members assigned here dur-ing the daytime and early evening hours. They are respon-sible for monitoring the residents and providing activities. We strongly encourage our residents to stay active during the day. We also have certified aides responsible for toileting our residents on a schedule. We try to avoid *accidents*, if possible. Why don't we go outside, and I'll introduce you to one of our residents."

As they moved outside, they encountered one of the residents involved in replanting a small gardenia bush. Catherine smiled as she said, "Hi, Eleanor, look at this beau-tiful plant."

"Well hello, I thought you weren't coming today."

"I know. I'm always late. I brought some friends to visit. This is Rachel and Peter."

Eleanor continued her gardening but looked up. "I think we met last time."

Peter didn't miss a beat. "We sure did, Eleanor. You have a great memory."

"Well I don't know about that, but I'm sure we've met."

Catherine seemed pleased with the encounter and said, "Eleanor, you look very happy today. Is there anything special going on?"

"No, I'm just waiting for John. He should be here soon."

"Well, no wonder you're so happy. Well, we better go, Eleanor. Thanks for taking care of our plants."

As they reentered the activity room, Catherine said, "I'm impressed, Peter. You catch on quick."

"I just thought about what she was probably thinking and tried to go along with it."

Catherine laughed and said, "Thus, the name New Perceptions. It's all about what they perceive. So you are communicating beyond the level of reasoning. By the way, John is Eleanor's husband. He passed away more than ten years ago. But it makes her happy to think he's coming. We respect that perception."

Rachel had been in deep thought. Her misty eyes met Catherine's as she spoke. "I talked like that with my grandpa when I was a little girl. It just came naturally. Why is it so difficult for this type of communication to be accepted?"

"It could be viewed as talking down to the residents, or even manipulating. Again it's about perception. It's important to utilize these techniques carefully and with respect. And of course there are times we choose not to engage with our residents' perceptions."

Rachel was confused. "Could you give me an example?"

"Well, if a resident has perceived that a certain staff member or another resident is trying to hurt him or her. We would not argue with them or try to convince them their perceived reality is wrong. But we would not engage in that perception either. We would acknowledge the perception and try a distraction technique. You have to know your residents well to know what works for them."

As they continued their tour, they passed a round table with a staff member and resident sitting next to one another. The staff member was busy filing the resident's fingernails. They were both relaxed and smiling as they visited.

Catherine stopped the tour as they reached the table. "We keep all our residents' nails short and filed. This is to prevent scratching and bacteria forming under the nail. We also encourage families to provide sweat clothing to wear. We suggest usually three or four sets of sweat suits. We have a sewing machine, and one of our activities is to modify the sweats with Velcro down the front and dress them up with buttons and collars. The material is inexpensive, warm, comfortable, and easy to wash. We use Velcro so they'll be easier to put on. Also, all residents wear tennis shoes with Velcro and comfortable socks."

Peter said, "Wow, you've thought of everything."

Catherine chuckled. "No, this is a continuous challenge. My hero, Florence Nightingale, said the human mind is no better understood today than it was two thousand years ago.

I'm willing to adjust in any way that helps the residents. For example, after the first week I realized we needed to go with finger foods as much as possible. Spoons and forks are so difficult for the residents to use. I contacted a nutritionist, and she helped us out."

They moved down a short hallway as they entered another circular area with doors surrounding.

"These are our patients' rooms. Every room is private. They are small but very comfortable."

Peter said, "I'm beginning to see how important it is to keep things simple."

Catherine responded, "Yes, and consistent. Our residents must feel like they can trust us. That is essential with communication. Our staff is very confident with the care they give."

Rachel looked at her watch and was amazed at how long they had been there. She was already in love with Catherine's facility and knew she would be back. "Catherine, I really need to take off, but I'd really like that number to contact Senator Green."

"Sure, just follow me back to my office."

As they walked, Peter gently touched Catherine's elbow. "Catherine, we can't thank you enough for this wonderful facility. Do you have any beds available?"

"I'm afraid not. We already have a waiting list. I can only hope we are helping to break a cycle. If administrators would be firm on communication techniques with no exceptions, things could improve. Rachel, I know your story will be enlightening, and I can't wait to read it."

"I appreciate that. I feel much more directed now that I've visited here. Thank you so much."

Catherine walked Peter and Rachel to the door. As they said their goodbyes, Catherine held on to Rachel's hand and said, "Senator Green is very serious about the harmful effects of legalized euthanasia. I hope you'll call him, Rachel."

"Don't worry. I intend to talk to him very soon."

Rachel and Peter walked to their cars. Peter asked, "What did you think about New Perceptions?"

"I'm thinking Grandpa James would have loved it."

"Is that your grandfather?"

"Yes, he died when I was a little girl. He was in a nursing home."

"So part of this story is personal."

"I think so."

"Well, call me if you need anything."

"I will. By the way, what did you think of Catherine?"

"I think I owe her a dinner," Peter responded with a wink.

8

Tim Duncan, private investigator, was sitting at his desk, which was littered with several empty coffee cups. His office held resemblance to someone's home after a hurricane has made a direct hit. Tim claimed he knew where everything was when in reality he could only guess and look. He opened an e-mail attachment marked *confidential*.

Tim grinned like a Cheshire cat as he said out loud, "Well, well, what have we here? Our medicine men are practicing more than healing. And it looks like a very profitable practice."

Tim picked up his phone and dialed Rachel's office number. Her answering machine picked up. "Rachel, this is your favorite PI. Call me when you get in tomorrow. I have something for you." Tim hung up, smiling his *I got you* grin.

Kyle and Rachel walked into Gino's Restaurant. Gino's was their favorite restaurant, considering the menu, pricing, and romantic ambience. They made a point of having one or two date nights a month. They were greeted by Brittney, who had been a hostess at Gino's for several years.

"Good evening, love birds. I saw your reservation and saved the booth in the back. Is that all right?"

Kyle smiled and said, "That would be perfect, Brittney. Thank you."

Brittney led them to a booth in the back. Kyle and Rachel scooted in close to one another. Kyle took Rachel's hand and lightly kissed it. "It's good to be alone with you."

"I know. This is wonderful."

"So did you visit that new Alzheimer's clinic?"

"Yes, it was amazing. It's called New Perceptions. All communication is done in the resident's perceived thoughts. In fact, some of the conversations sounded pretty bizarre!"

"Is that a good thing or a bad thing?"

"Surprisingly it's a very good thing. They don't use baby talk or degrading tones; just, sometimes it's funny. I think the sense of humor helps keep things, ah, happy."

"Sounds like you're sold."

"I am. I really wish Grandpa James could have been in a place like that. He would've loved it."

"I bet he would have. It sounds like you're reaching a resolution to your euthanasia questions."

"I think so. In fact, I'm convinced that innocent people use euthanasia out of desperation. I mean, there are some evil people who'll use it to get an early inheritance or something like that. But I think most people are convinced it's the only dignified thing to do."

Kyle took a sip of water and asked, "Well, what's your next step? Are you ready to write your story?"

"Not yet. I have an investigator checking on a couple of things about Peaceful Transitions. My gut tells me there's something I need to know."

Kyle quickly added, "And like any good reporter, your gut is usually right."

Rachel leaned over and planted a kiss on Kyle's cheek. "Thanks, honey. Also, there's a Senator Green who has asked a Senate commission to conduct a hearing on legalized euthanasia. I'm going to contact him and hopefully meet him."

"This is going to be a great story. I can feel it."

"Thanks; from your mouth to God's ears! Also, there might be a romance brewing between Peter and Catherine."

"No kidding. Never a boring moment in your life, Rachel."

"Nope."

The waitress appeared, wearing her black slacks and white collared shirt, the Gino's standard uniform for decades. Kyle ordered the lasagna and Rachel the eggplant parmesan. Rachel followed up on her thought. "My life is definitely going to be interesting for now."

Rachel entered her office with a smile of confidence and determination. She slid her purse into her lower drawer and punched the play button on her answering machine. It was Tim Duncan's message to return his call ASAP. Rachel wondered why Tim hadn't tried her on her cell phone and instinctively pulled it out of her purse. Her phone was still off from the night before. She had mentally given herself permission to take the night off and enjoy the date with her husband. Rachel returned Tim's call.

"Hi, Tim, this is Rachel. What have you got?"

"It seems our Dr. McKay has become a very wealthy man of late."

Rachel's eyes widened. "How wealthy are we talking?"

"Wealthy enough to stash 1.3 million in a secret account."

"Unbelievable. Great work, Tim. How'd you find it?"

"Now now, Rachel, I have my ways. And that's not all. Seems a couple of the board members for Peaceful Transitions are old partners of the good doctor. They're all geriatric doctors. I'll send you the list."

"Yeah, that'd be great. I owe you one, Tim. Thanks."

"Just get them, Rachel. This is one of the worst things I've ever seen someone do for money. And I've seen a lot."

"Hopefully the facts will do just that. Bye, Tim."

"See ya."

Rachel walked to the fax machine. She pulled out the fax from Tim. She read the fax while slowly walking back to her desk. She almost missed her chair as she said out loud, "Oh no!" The third name on the list of board of directors read *Dr.*

Tom Kramer. Rachel remembered that Dr. Kramer was poor Gracie's physician. Rachel called Tim back.

"Hello, Rachel," Tim said when he picked up.

"Honestly, Tim, I'll never get used to caller ID. I need another favor. I spotted a familiar name on the list you sent over. Dr. Tom Kramer. I met his patient's husband at the clinic. Maybe you could track down other patients he's referred to the clinic and see what they have to say."

"I'll get right on it."

Rachel sat for almost an hour reflecting on her encounter with Walter as well as Peter's perspective on suffering. She was beginning to see how easy it could be to twist someone's suffering into a hefty bank account. The ring of her phone broke her concentration.

"This is Rachel Scott."

"Hello, Rachel, this is Senator Green returning your call."

Rachel sat up straight as if he were in the same room. "Thank you, Senator. I was hoping to set up a meeting with you to discuss legalized euthanasia issues."

"Yes, I've talked to Catherine at New Perceptions. I'm not sure if Catherine told you that my mother is a resident at New Perceptions."

"No, but of course it isn't surprising that someone like Catherine would maintain confidentiality."

"Well, that is one of the many characteristics I admire about Catherine. Can you meet tomorrow? I plan to be in town for the day."

"Of course; that would be great. I'll see you then."

Rachel hung up and couldn't remember a time when she had been more excited.

9

The next day was a beautiful, sunny day in Phoenix. Rachel sat on a park bench awaiting Senator Green. She loved the park and often spent her lunches sitting at one of the picnic tables and absorbing the beauty there. She spotted a tall, slightly overweight man approaching her. She instinctively knew it was Senator Green.

"Hello, you must be Rachel Scott. Please forgive my tardiness."

Rachel stood and extended her hand. "It's perfectly fine. I'm enjoying the sunshine. I'm pleased you're in town and able to meet with me."

Senator Green glanced at his watch as he said, "I have to

admit I'm pressed for time, but after talking to Catherine, I felt it was important for us to connect."

"Did Catherine tell you I was writing a piece on Peaceful Transitions?"

"Yes, she did. We had a nice visit while I sat with Mom."

"How's your mother doing?"

"She's getting along well. It's such a relief to know she's in the care of people who understand her condition."

"I can imagine. I'd like to talk about your push for an investigation into legalized euthanasia."

"I was against legalized euthanasia from the get-go. I was sick about the opening of Peaceful Transitions. We've finally gotten a commission together to investigate the goings-on in the clinic. It's been a slow process, though."

"I understand it's been really difficult to bring this to a federal level."

"It sure has. Most of my peers feel things like this are best left up to the individual states. Usually I agree, but there's something about this one that sickens me."

Rachel handed Senator Green a manila envelope and said, "I obtained some information that might be of interest to you. I'm sure you already know some of it."

Senator Green opened the envelope and examined the contents. His left eyebrow lifted as he spoke to Rachel. "I knew the clinic was for-profit, but I never knew this kind of money was generated."

"It's mind-boggling. The name highlighted, Dr. Kramer, is a geriatric physician who refers his patients to Peaceful Transitions."

"How do you know that?"

"I spoke with an elderly gentleman at the clinic. His wife had just been euthanized. He was pretty distraught and told me his story."

"I'd call that a chance meeting."

"No kidding. I haven't gone any further with this. I'm sure there are other clients who have been referred by board members."

Senator Green replaced the documents in the manila envelope as he responded, "No doubt. Have you checked the tax returns on Dr. McKay? Perhaps some of this money stashed in offshore accounts was forgotten?"

"No. I haven't gotten that far."

"Well, why don't you leave that up to me and my contacts?" Senator Green stood up and announced, "I've got to get going, Rachel. You have made my day, though."

Rachel smiled and said, "Likewise, Senator."

Senator Green started walking off and stopped abruptly. He turned around to face Rachel. Rachel had begun walking in the opposite direction. Senator Green called out. "Excuse me, Rachel."

Rachel faced Senator Green. "Yes?"

"Watch your back. These men are smart and greedy. Be careful."

"Thank you. You do the same."

On the drive back to her office, Rachel mentally tried to outline her story. She understood the importance of reporting all sides of the story. She struggled to find a way to report on the aspect of suffering caregivers making the decision for euthanasia without sounding judgmental.

She walked into the office and caught sight of Rusty. He was in his office on the phone, and she could tell he wasn't happy. Rachel kept her eye on him until he hung up. Rusty looked up and motioned her to come into his office. Rachel walked slowly into his office and took a seat across from Rusty's desk.

"Hi, Rusty, what's going on?"

"Look, Rachel, I just got off the phone with Mr. Ennis." Mr. Ennis, Rusty's boss, had been in charge of the magazine since conception. He had learned how to manage every outside and inside source that tried to influence his magazine. He seldom compromised.

"So how's the big boss doing?"

"Honestly, he's concerned about your story. Seems some of the physicians you questioned have friends in high places."

Rachel sat straight up and said, "Don't tell me he wants me to back off."

"Not exactly. He was talking more like we should table the story."

Rachel ejected from her seat, now raising her voice loud enough to catch the attention of her peers. "No! No way, Rusty. I haven't had a chance to tell you what Tim dug up. Hold on and let me get you the information."

Rachel hurried to her desk and pulled out the documents Tim had faxed her. She almost tripped on her way back to Rusty's office. "Here, look at this."

Rachel handed Rusty the documents as she took a deep breath.

After a moment of perusal, Rusty said, "Okay. I can see why you're so worked up. Tell you what. Why don't you keep working on the story, and I'll see what I can do. But I can't promise anything."

"Thanks. I owe you."

Rachel returned to her desk, her heart racing. She answered her ringing phone in a daze.

"Rachel Scott speaking."

A muffled male voice spoke. "If you know what's good for you, you'll scrap the euthanasia story."

"Who is this?"

"Get off the story, or things will happen to your family."

"I don't know who this is, but your threats don't scare me."

"Consider this your last warning."

The phone clicked as the strange man hung up. Rachel stared at the phone as her breathing became heavy. Then she grabbed her purse and ran out of the building.

Rachel drove her familiar path home at double speed. She noticed the front door was open as she slammed on the brakes in the driveway. Rachel rushed through the house calling out the names of her family. She spotted Kyle through the patio door mowing the back lawn. Rachel raced to her husband.

"Kyle, Kyle, where are the girls? The front door is open. I can't find them."

Kyle had already cut the mower's engine. "What is wrong with you? You're acting crazy."

"Where are the girls, Kyle?"

"They're inside playing. What's wrong with you?"

"They're not in the house. I looked and called out for them."

Rachel ran back inside and started calling out their names again. Kyle, still bewildered, followed Rachel inside. As Rachel ran downstairs, Sarah and Laura walked through the front door.

"Oh my goodness. Where have you been?"

Sarah looked puzzled and scared. "What's wrong, Mom?"

Rachel's voice was shaking now as she screamed, "I asked, where have you been? You aren't allowed to leave this house without permission."

Laura answered tearfully, "We were looking outside and saw Cindy next door playing with a kitten. Dad was mowing the lawn, and we couldn't get his attention."

"So you just decided it would be all right to go next door without telling anyone. What's wrong with you girls?"

Kyle stood watching as Rachel became increasingly upset. Both girls were now crying. Kyle intervened. "Sarah, take Laura upstairs; we'll be up shortly."

"All right, Dad. I'm really sorry."

"It's fine, Sarah. Go upstairs now."

Sarah and Laura went upstairs to their room. Kyle took Rachel's hand and led her to the sofa.

Kyle spoke softly. "Rachel, would you please tell me what is going on?"

"It's nothing. I just panicked when I couldn't find the girls."

"That's not like you, so how about the whole truth?"

Rachel melted into Kyle's arms and cried.

"Please don't go crazy, but I received a call at work today."

"A threatening call?"

"Yes. It was a man, I think. He said I should drop the euthanasia story or my family would be in danger."

Kyle hugged her for comfort. "No wonder you were so scared. What did Rusty say?"

"I didn't tell him. He had told me earlier that my story was in jeopardy. I wasn't sure if the call was legit, so I didn't want to risk upsetting him."

"Rachel, you have to tell Rusty. He has a right to know. On top of that, I'm not sure *I* want you to continue the story now either."

"I'll tell Rusty but not yet. Kyle, this story is too important. Not only for me, but all those poor people who believe they're dying for dignity."

"I don't know, Rachel. The stakes are running high."

"Okay, what if the girls stay with Mom until the story's finished?"

"I definitely agree with that, but what about *your* safety?"

Rachel suddenly felt very tired. She felt sick to her stomach thinking about being separated from her daughters. "Kyle, I need to do this. I know the risk and sacrifice involved. Please help me do this."

With a deep sigh, Kyle said, "You win, but we need some ground rules. You need to call me at a certain time every day. Also carry your mace with you at all times."

"I'll do it. Thank you so much, Kyle."

Rachel and Kyle walked upstairs and entered Sarah's room. Sarah was sitting on her bed with Laura snuggled close to her. Kyle stopped in the doorway as Rachel approached the girls.

"I'm really sorry, girls. I just got scared when you weren't home."

Sarah quickly answered, "We won't do that again, Mom."

Laura had forgotten they were in trouble. She could only think about the very thing that had gotten them into this mess. "Mom, you should see Cindy's kitten. It's so cute!"

"Maybe I'll see it soon. Listen, how would you like to spend a few days with Grandma?"

Laura exclaimed, "Yeah! We could go to the beach."

Sarah looked concerned. "It's too cold to go to the beach. And what about school?"

Kyle came closer as he spoke. "Sarah, you can wear a sweatshirt to the beach. Mom will talk to your teachers and arrange things."

"Why do you want us to go to Grandma's?"

Once again Rachel was faced with the reality that Sarah was mature beyond her years. Rachel sat on the bed next to Sarah as she said, "Look, I'm going to be working really hard on my story. I could have some really late nights. And Dad is pretty busy right now. We just think it would be the best option, and besides, Grandma really misses you."

Kyle smiled broadly. "I hope she won't spoil you too much. You know, with chocolate ice cream, cookies, and the mall!"

Laura screamed, "Yay! Let's go!"

Rachel ran her fingers through Sarah's hair. "Sarah, are you with this?"

"Yes, Mom, it'll be fun."

"I'll call Grandma tonight. I love you both very much. Thank you for helping Mom."

That night Rachel called Linda and arranged for the visit. Linda was thrilled at the thought of having her granddaughters to herself. It never seemed to occur to her that something was very wrong with her daughter. Kyle had decided to get a substitute for his classes and fly the girls himself. A discussion took place whether the girls could make the direct flight alone. He hated to leave Rachel but felt he needed to fill Linda in so she would take extra care watching the girls.

The next morning was chaotic as Kyle packed the car. Sarah and Laura were excited about the trip and couldn't decide how much they wanted to take with them. Kyle was shoving suitcases, blankets, and pillows, into their SUV.

"Hey, girls, I think we have enough to spend a year at Grandma's."

Rachel stood with her arms crossed. She was concerned. Rachel kissed the girls as they settled into their seats. "I'm going to miss you guys."

Kyle walked around the car and wrapped his arms around Rachel. "You're going to talk to Rusty today?"

"Yes, I promise."

"I don't like leaving you here."

"Don't worry about me. I'll be careful. I don't really believe anyone wants to hurt *me*. They just want the story scratched."

"How can you say that, Rachel? These people take lives for a living."

"You're right. I guess I should take this seriously."

"Keep your cell phone on. Check in with me as much as possible."

"I promise. I love you."

"I love you too."

Rachel hated watching her family drive off. She choked back the tears as she walked back to her house. She looked around her quiet home and decided to wash the morning dishes. Halfway through she picked up the phone and called Rusty.

"Hi, Rusty, this is Rachel. I'm going to be in late today."

"Are you okay? You sound like something's wrong."

"Well I've been better, but I'll talk to you when I get there."

Rachel walked upstairs and jumped in the shower. She felt somewhat refreshed after a long shower.

As she walked out of the master bathroom with wet hair and wearing a robe, she picked up her purse. She sat on her bed, took out the picture of her grandpa, and allowed the tears to flow as she looked at it.

Rachel said to herself, "Grandpa, you've always been my hero. I'm doing this story for you. That's what will get me through this now."

10

Rachel parked her car in the parking lot at Phoenix Community Church. She walked through the church into Peter Wade's office. Peter was busy preparing for his sermon and was pulling a book off one of his many shelves. Peter had rows of religious books, including different interpretations of the Bible. Peter looked up and saw Rachel standing in his doorway.

"Well, isn't this a pleasant surprise."

"I hope so. How are you doing?"

"Fantastic. What about you?"

"Not as well. Do you have a minute?"

Peter placed the book on his desk and pulled a chair out and motioned for Rachel to sit down. "I'll make one for you."

"Thank you. I'm feeling I might need your advice or maybe prayers."

"You already have them, but is there something in particular?"

"Yes, I've been getting threatening phone calls about the euthanasia story."

"Rachel, I'm so sorry. What can I do?"

"Continued prayers would be great. I'm also wondering if I'm too emotionally invested in the story. I mean, if I'm walking straight into danger because I'm so driven to expose the truth about Peaceful Transitions."

"I understand your concern, but sometimes we have to face danger and push forward in order for change to take place. Do you believe God is with you, Rachel?"

"Yes, and Grandpa James, and even Gracie, Walter's wife."

"Then no matter what, God will bless you for being a voice to those who can't speak for themselves."

"Thank you, Peter."

"You're welcome." Peter opened his drawer and pulled out an envelope. He passed the envelope to Rachel and said, "One of our members gave this to me yesterday. She wrote this memoir for her mother. I think it was therapeutic for her. Anyway, it seemed like something that would go along with your story. I asked if I could give a copy to you, and she said it was all right."

Rachel took the letter out and noticed it was printed on beautiful paper. She began to read some of the most pro-found memories a daughter could have. Rachel whispered the first part of the letter out loud before falling into silence as she read.

> I walked into Mom's room feeling the love that surrounded her. It was day twenty-three, and my daughter and son were sitting on the edge of her hospital bed, which had been delivered on day one. The room was filled with fresh flowers, and the smell of scented lotion permeated the room. Every day I softened Mom's skin with one of her favorite scented lotions. I decorated her room so it would be pleasing and a peaceful place for rest.
>
> As I looked upon the scene, I remembered thinking that my life had taken a surreal turn. How could it be possible that my strong, independent mother could be driven to such a bedridden state? My mother had raised her children, two of her sisters, and a grandson with as much dignity and grace a women could have. Now she had reached her final days. At times the reality of that literally took my breath away.
>
> It was a journey like being lost in a deep forest, and in a desperate attempt to find our way out occasionally a light would shine. But this journey was cruel in that the closer we came to the light the darker and more lost we became. In fact, most spirits would have slipped into dark despair or broken completely. For sure mine would have if not for the eternal character of my mother.

As Rachel finished reading the letter she looked up at Peter and said, "This is amazing, especially the way they invested in the dying process so it would not be so overwhelming."

"It's true there are many ways to prepare for death if the dying can face the inevitable. The one thing that stood out to me was the conflicting emotions of the family. I see that all the time."

"You mean where some of the family are ready to let go and others can't."

"Yes, I believe this mom knew she could spend her last days dying in peace with her daughter. That, to me, is dying with dignity. Dr. McKay and his group have twisted the minds of the dying into thinking suicide is the only dignified death."

"This will help with my story. I better go now and face my boss."

"Problems?"

"No, not really. I promised Kyle I'd fill Rusty in on the threatening phone call. I'm not sure how he'll react, that's all."

"Another thing I'll have to add to my prayer list."

"You just might run out of paper! By the way, anything new with Catherine?"

Peter grinned and said, "Okay, I admit, I'm completely smitten."

Rachel's instincts had been right on again. "Is Catherine your first love, Peter?"

"No. I was engaged a long time ago. We were, as the Bible says, 'unequally yoked.' Since then I have been married to the church."

Rachel couldn't help thinking what a lucky lady Catherine

would be. Peter broke the silence as he stretched his arms and asked, "So, should I ask her out?"

"You're a fool if you don't."

"It's settled then. I'll call her today. Wish me luck."

Rachel left Phoenix Community Church feeling renewed. She was thinking about the memoir she had read when her cell phone started ringing.

"Hello."

"Hey, Rachel, this is Tim. I just stopped by your office to see you."

"Hi, Tim. I'm headed to the office now."

"Great! I'll stay put right here in Rusty's office until you get here."

Rachel walked into her office building and spotted Tim and Rusty laughing. She smiled at the sight of them. They had been friends for a long time. Rachel was thankful they accepted her as an equal. Tim greeted her with a big hug.

Rusty said, "Well, it's about time you got here."

"Sorry it's so late. It was important."

Tim added, "Little lady, I have some important news for you." Rachel smiled broadly as Tim talked to her. "Remember you asked me to check into other patients of Dr. Kramer."

"Yes, did you find someone?"

"I sure did. But this patient is a former patient of Dr. Kramer. He didn't exactly like Dr. Kramer's referral."

Rachel moved to the edge of her seat and said, "Really! Do tell."

"His name is Gerald Sides. He has cancer of the colon.

He's under hospice care now. About a month after his diagnosis, he became depressed. He's a widower and lives alone. That's when Dr. Kramer referred him to the clinic."

"Amazing! He was referred, just like that."

"Yep. Gerald said he went to an appointment at the clinic. He met with Doc McKay and a social worker. He said the whole thing was a "scam" to take his money. Gerald is my kind of man."

"Sounds like it. Do you think he'd let me interview him for my story?"

"I know he would because I asked him. Here's his phone number." Tim gave Rachel the white paper with Gerald's phone number.

Rusty leaned back in his chair and put his hands behind his head. "Tim, we don't pay you enough."

Tim chuckled. "That's for sure. Anyway Gerald said his time is limited, so don't wait too long."

Rachel said, "Gerald sounds like my kind of man too. Ah, Rusty, there's something I need to tell you."

Rusty's eyebrows rose as he said, "What is it?"

"Don't go ballistic, but yesterday I got a threatening phone call."

Rusty shot out of his chair as he yelled, "You what! Rachel, you know you can't keep that kind of thing quiet!"

"I know. It's just you said Mr. Ennis was considering pulling my story. I was afraid if you knew, that would seal the fate of my story."

"So why are you telling me today?"

"When I got home yesterday, I couldn't find the girls, and it was pretty awful."

Rusty almost pulled his hair out. "Darn it, Rachel."

"It's all right, Rusty. They had gone over to a neighbor without permission, but I really panicked."

"I can imagine what Kyle's thinking."

"That's why I'm coming clean with you. I promised Kyle. But Kyle knows how important this story is to me. He took the girls to Mom's house in Carmel."

Tim had listened intently. He finally said, "Well, that's smart thinking. Listen, I'm willing to keep an eye on you."

Rusty said, "Back up the truck, Tim. This is getting serious."

"Rusty, we've had wacko phone calls before. We just need to be careful," Tim said.

Rachel was thankful for Tim's support, and she intended to use it. "Tim's right. We can't give up now. Please, Rusty, I need your support."

Rusty looked at Tim with intense eyes as he said, "You better keep a close watch on her. I'm not kidding."

"Don't worry. I'm her new shadow."

Rachel breathed a sigh of relief. "I've got work to do now. I'll be leaving around six tonight, Tim. Kyle will be home late tomorrow night."

"Gotcha. Don't worry. You won't even know I'm around."

Rusty interjected, "I'm going along with this, but I don't like it."

Rachel decided to make a quick exit to her desk. She called Kyle to check in. "Hi, honey. How was the flight?"

"Pretty good, we just landed in San Jose."

"So the girls are doing well."

"Yeah, they slept most of the way."

"That's good. I'm at the office now. Tim Duncan is here, and I told him and Rusty about the call."

"Thank God. So what did Rusty say?"

"He's not happy but felt better when Tim offered to be my personal bodyguard."

"That makes me feel better too."

"So anyway, for now I have the green light to continue with my story. I really feel like pouring my heart out now. I'm ready to put my story together."

"Well, good! I do feel better knowing Tim is around. I'm at the rental car counter, so I'll try to call you later."

"Give Mom my love and kiss the girls."

"You got it. Bye, honey."

Rachel got busy typing at her computer. Her story began to flow. She began to visualize Walter at Peaceful Transitions and then see the residents at New Perceptions engaging with the staff, smiling and laughing. She remembered the beautiful tribute she had read just that day of a daughter to her dying mother. She was resolved to tell a story that could reach society and leave it with a sense of true dignity about dying. Rachel was at peace.

II

Rachel had worked for several hours straight and looked up to see the clock reading six p.m. She turned off her computer and headed for her car. In the parking garage, she thought she heard something. She nervously opened her car door and jumped inside. As she drove home, she noticed a car following her. She sped up and hurriedly pulled into her garage. Rachel ran inside as the garage door was closing. She realized her cell phone had been ringing. Now her house phone started ringing. She was breathing so hard she could hardly answer the phone.

"Hello."

"Rachel, this is Tim. I tried to call you on your cell to let you know it was me following you home."

"Oh my goodness. I completely forgot. I have to admit, I was really scared."

"I'm parked across the street. Can you see me?"

Rachel pulled the window curtain back and saw his car as Tim waved out the window. "Yes, I see you. I'm safe and sound now."

"I'll stay put for a while. Good night, Rachel."

"Thank you, Tim. Good night."

Kyle was thankful for the easy flight. By the time he rented a car and drove more than an hour from the San Jose airport, it was dinner time. Linda rushed around getting dinner on the table.

"You look exhausted. Are you sure you can't stay a couple of days?" asked Linda.

"No, I need to get back. We sure appreciate you watching the girls."

"No need for thanks, Kyle. I'm just as excited as they are, and we have big plans."

Kyle laughed and said, "I can imagine."

Linda and Kyle made their way to the living area and sat down. Linda gave Kyle a long look.

"Is Rachel all right?"

"Yes, she is. You know Rachel has always been able to see things others can't. It amazes me, her insight on some issues."

"She was always like that. Even as a child she seemed

to be a voice for others. But what does that have to do with anything?"

"Rachel was assigned a story about legalized euthanasia. She met with the director of the first legalized clinic in Oregon and has had an odd discernment from the start. She listened to her heart and followed leads that have upset some people."

"Is she in danger?"

"She did get a threatening phone call."

"What! Kyle, I don't like this."

"I know, but Rachel doesn't want to back down. We have a private investigator watching her."

"Well, now I know why you're so anxious to get home. I can't imagine how much the flights must have cost."

Kyle hoped he didn't sound harsh when he said, "Linda, right now, money is the least of my worries."

Kyle gave Linda a quick hug to soothe any potential damage. "Don't worry. Rachel's doing the right thing."

Senator Green finished his coffee and glanced at his watch. He had an early meeting at his Washington, DC office. He folded his paper and tucked it under his arm. He exited Yong's coffee shop and waited at the corner light. He had started to cross the street when he thought he heard a car racing down the street toward him. He started to run, but it was too late. The car actually sped up and sent him flying through the air a good twenty feet. He hit the ground hard as the large, black car turned the corner and disappeared. Senator Green lay on the ground, not moving, as the owner of Yong's coffee shop called 911.

Rachel leaned against the couch sipping her morning coffee. She was enjoying the morning news on television when there was a break in the programming. They reported that a hit-and-run accident had occurred in Washington, DC, involving Senator Green. The incident had occurred early in the morning hours. The news reminded the viewers that Senator Green had served for twenty years and currently was heading up a special committee investigating legalized euthanasia. The senator's condition was unknown at this time.

Rachel spilled her coffee everywhere as she rushed to the telephone. She dialed the number for New Perceptions.

"Hello, this is Rachel Scott. Could I please speak with Catherine Perez?"

The voice at the other end replied, "Just a moment please."

"Hello, Rachel. I guess you've have heard about Senator Green."

"Yes, I just saw the broadcast. Do you know anything?"

"I have an inside source, and from what I'm able to find out, he's in pretty bad shape."

"Oh no! Have you heard who might have been responsible?"

"No."

"Thanks, Catherine. I'll see what I can find out when I get to work."

"Please call me if you hear anything, and I'll do the same."

"That sounds good. Talk to you later."

The moment Rachel hung the phone up, it was ringing again. It was Kyle.

"Hi, honey. Have you heard about Senator Green?"

"Yes, I just saw it on the news."

"I'm worried about you. Is Tim around?"

Rachel looked outside. "Yes, he's outside across the street in his car."

"I think you should go straight to the office and stay there."

"That's probably a good idea. I have so much work to do anyway. Are you on your way home?"

"Yes, I left early this morning. I've been worried about you since I heard the morning news. I've checked the rental car in and now I'm waiting standby for the next flight out. I think you should give the girls and your mom a call. I told your mom about the threat, and she's concerned."

"I'll call them right now. See you soon."

"Okay. Love you."

"I love you too."

Rachel dialed the phone number to her mother's house. She was surprised when Sarah answered the telephone.

"Hello, this is the King residence."

"Hi, Sarah, it's Mom."

"Hi, Mom, Grandma lets me answer her phone and even take messages."

"That's very good, Sarah. How are you?"

"I'm fine, but I really miss you."

"I know. Are you having fun with Grandma?"

"Yes. We're going to the aquarium tomorrow and shopping today."

"I wish I were there. It sounds like fun. Honey, I need to get to work now. Give Laura a big kiss for me."

"I will, Mom. I love you."

"I love you too, Sarah. Bye now."

Rachel hung up and wanted to cry. She didn't allow herself to go there but rushed upstairs to brush her teeth. Before she walked out the door, she stopped and closed her eyes, saying a silent prayer for Senator Green and his family.

Rachel entered her office with Tim on her heels. Tim said, "Rachel, what's your take on this Senator Green thing?"

Rachel turned around "I'm not sure right now. I'm hoping it was an accident and the driver just panicked."

"Fat chance! He has a Senate hearing scheduled next month. More than likely someone wanted to shut him up."

"I guess you're paid to be suspicious."

"Well, so are you. Anyway, we need to be really careful, Rachel. What's your schedule today?"

"I'll be right here typing my heart out. I'll even order lunch in if it would make you feel better."

"It would."

Rusty joined Rachel and Tim. "It would me too. This is getting crazy, Rachel. I just talked to my source in DC. It seems that Senator Green had received some threatening phone calls too. He was advised to hire a bodyguard and refused. My source tells me he's conscious now. He didn't see who hit him, but there were a couple of witnesses who got a make on the car. I guess the senator's pretty banged up."

"Thank God he's going to make it. I wonder if any information turned up about Dr. McKay's IRS returns."

Rusty said, "Believe me, if the good doctor has stolen from the IRS, we'll hear about it soon enough."

Rachel looked hopeful. She said, "Hopefully before the hearing next month. I told Catherine at New Perceptions I'd give her a call if I heard anything. I better do that."

Tim said, "I'm going to leave for a while. I have a friend watching the building while I'm gone. Call me on my cell if you need anything."

Rusty replied, "You bet. Thanks again, Tim."

Tim started to walk away then turned to ask Rachel a question. "Hey, Rachel, did you get a hold of Gerald Sides yet?"

"No, I plan to call him tomorrow. I really look forward to that phone call."

"That's good. Now be a good girl and stay put."

"Yes, sir!"

The room was quiet except for the occasional beeping of machines. Senator Green lay in his hospital bed with bandages covering his head, ribs, left femur, and left shoulder. He had been in and out of consciousness the past hour. His wife, Nancy, was sitting at his bedside. She looked over to the door to see a familiar face. It was Senator John Price, a friend of her husband's for more than twenty-five years.

"Hi, John, it's good to see you."

"You too, Nancy. It's been too long. How's my friend doing?"

"He seems to be regaining consciousness. He's pretty sedated, though."

"Do you think I could try to talk to him?"

"You can try. Maybe I'll grab some coffee. Would you like some?"

"Yeah, that would be great, Nancy. Thank you."

John Price took the seat Nancy had left beside Senator Green's bed.

Senator Price gently touched his friend's shoulder and said, "Hi, Jim, can you talk?"

Senator Green opened his eyes slightly and focused in on his longtime friend. He answered, "Yes, but I'm really cloudy. Do they know who did this?"

"We're working on it. The FBI's investigating. I'm glad you reported the calls. My gut tells me they could be linked."

"I got a call from the IRS late yesterday afternoon. They're going to file charges against McKay for tax evasion."

"No kidding! That's great news, Jim. It should help our case during the euthanasia hearings."

Senator Green was beginning to drift off again. He managed to say, "John, call Rachel Scott from *Situational Life* Magazine and tell her we need her story out ASAP."

"I'll take care of it. Now you just rest."

Nancy walked back into the room and handed Senator Price his coffee. He stood up.

Nancy asked, "Did he wake up?"

"Yes, for a minute. Listen, thanks for the coffee, but I've got to run."

"Thanks for coming by, John. I know how much Jim thinks of you and your good work."

"I appreciate that. I'll call or stop by later tonight."

Rachel was sleeping soundly in her bed when she was awakened by a noise. She opened her eyes to see a man standing over her. She was startled and gasped loudly. She heard her husband's voice.

"It's me, honey. I'm sorry I scared you. I just talked to Tim and told him to go home tonight."

Rachel wrapped her arms tightly around Kyle and said, "I'm so glad you're home."

"Yeah, I'm glad to be home."

"I talked to Sarah this morning. She misses me."

"I know, honey. Well, your mom's taking them to the aquarium tomorrow. That should be fun."

"Yes, they'll love that. Come to bed."

"I'll be right there after a quick shower."

Rachel snuggled back into bed, so glad to have her husband home. Soon Kyle crawled into bed and took his wife into his arms.

"Kyle whispered, "So what's the word on your story?"

"It's my best work yet! I have one more interview, then I'll complete my masterpiece."

"Then maybe we can have a normal life again."

Rachel really felt for her husband. It had to be difficult to support her and also so much want the whole thing to go away. "I'm sorry this story has been so complex."

"I love you, Rachel, and right now I just want to kiss you."

"In that case I'll shut up."

Dr. McKay and Dr. Kramer sat in the plush office at Peaceful Transitions drinking their morning coffee. Neither of them looked well. They had problems that weren't being handled properly.

Dr. Kramer finally said, "I don't feel too confident about the Senate hearing. I still think we need a caregiver to testify on our behalf."

Dr. McKay was clearly irritated with his partner. "Oh

yeah, which one should we pick? Chris Jenkins? I can hear him now saying, 'I am in complete support of euthanasia. If it weren't for Peaceful Transitions, I would still be in the streets drinking the cheap stuff. Instead, thanks to them, Dad got an early trip to heaven, and I'm living in an upscale condo drinking the best bourbon available.' That ought to set those Senators straight."

"You don't have to be difficult about this, Bill. There are legitimate families that could testify."

"You know the score, Tom. Our families are vulnerable. It would be easy for Senator Green to have them sobbing in no time."

"I thought we took care of Senator Green."

This time Dr. McKay was unable to restrain his emotions. He slammed his cup on his desk, spilling the black coffee everywhere. "Shut the hell up, Tom. Don't mention that again."

"Bill, I think you should just calm down. We can take care of the hearing ourselves. My contact in the governor's office assures me that this hearing means nothing. It's basically to pacify Senator Green. We'll handle this."

"Well, forgive me if I don't feel very confident in our contacts right now."

12

Rachel walked into her office confidently. She knew her story would be finished soon. She took off her coat and put away her purse. She opened her top desk drawer and took out Gerald Sides's phone number. She dialed and hoped he felt well enough to answer some questions. Gerald answered on the second ring.

"Hello, this is Rachel Scott with *Situational Life* Magazine. I got your phone number from Tim Duncan. Do you remember him?"

"I sure do. Tim is quite a fellow. I guess you're calling about Dr. Kramer."

"Yes, I am. I'm working on a story about euthanasia and Peaceful Transitions. Do you mind if I ask you a few questions?"

"Not at all. I told Tim I'd answer anything you wanted. I can't believe I almost became a victim of that place."

"I'm going to be taping our conversation. Is that all right with you?"

"Sure, I don't mind."

Rachel clicked on the recorder and began, "Gerald, could you tell me about Dr. Kramer's referral to Peaceful Transitions?"

"I was a patient of Dr. Kramer's, and hospice wasn't involved then. My pain was pretty bad, and I wasn't sure how much I could stand. Dr. Kramer prescribed Vicodin for the pain and said that was about the strongest medication he could recommend."

"So, you asked Dr. Kramer for something stronger and he refused?"

"He didn't really refuse. He just said that was the strongest until I was at the end. He said that's when I could use morphine."

"I see. Then what happened?"

"Well, I became really depressed. I just stayed in bed and cried a lot. My neighbor found me one day and took me in to see Dr. Kramer."

"So you agreed to go with your neighbor to Dr. Kramer's office."

"Yes. I told him I wished it would hurry up and get over. I meant my death. I was hurting and didn't have much hope. I didn't even understand what was happening. That's when he said he knew of a place that might help me out."

"Peaceful Transitions?"

"That's right."

"Gerald, did you know it was a euthanasia clinic?"

"Not at first. I thought it was a hospice hospital. That maybe I was near the end and they would help me with the pain. Then I went over there and met with this social worker. Boy was she ever a piece of work."

"How so?"

"She told me I should take control over my death. That I could end it while I still had some dignity left. That basically there was no need to suffer when I had a choice to stop the suffering. She sounded too much like a used car salesman for me."

Rachel laughed then asked, "So what did you do?"

"I got out of there as quick as I could. I used to run track in high school, and I came close to breaking my record!"

"I'm sure you did. I wish I could have seen it. So did you ever say anything to Dr. Kramer?"

"No. I called another doctor I had seen years before. He referred me to hospice. Since then everything has been under control. I still have a hard time eating, but the pain is controlled better. Also, they aren't afraid to talk to me about dying and what to expect."

"I'm so glad. Can you think of anything else that might help me with my story?"

"No, except my new doctor made a comment that he wished to God they would close that place down. He said something about keeping his Hippocratic Oath."

"Thanks, Gerald. If I think of anything else, I'll let you know."

"You bet. Oh, would you mind mailing me a copy of your story?"

Rachel smiled as she thought how special this man made her feel. Honestly, for him thinking of her story in his frail condition. "That would be my pleasure. Goodbye, Gerald."

Rachel put the phone down and choked back the tears as she began to type.

It was late in the afternoon when Kyle started to leave the campus. He was exhausted as he cranked his car. He pulled out his cell phone and noticed a missed call from Rachel. A flood of emotions struck him while he quickly hit the dial button.

"Hello, you handsome man."

"Hi, honey, are you all right?"

"Everything's fine. I just wanted to hear your voice."

"Well, with everything going on, I can't help worrying about you."

"I'm sorry, Kyle."

"It's okay. Where are you with your story?"

"I'm going to finish it today, or should I say, tonight. Are you leaving work now?"

"Yeah, I spent half the class time getting students back to our routine. Amazing how the mice will play when the cat's away."

"Yes, and speaking of that, I wonder if our little mice are playing right now."

"You really miss them, huh."

"More than you can imagine. That's one of the reasons I'm committed to finishing this story today. The other is, Rusty said he would personally break my neck if I didn't!"

Kyle chuckled. "Nothing like physical violence for incentive! I'm going to head home now. Why don't you call me when you're finished, and I'll come get you? We can go out and celebrate."

"That sounds like a great idea."

13

Rachel pulled the last pages away from the printer. She clipped all the pages together as she read the cover page one last time. *"Dignity in Question: Is there ever dignity in death?" by Rachel Scott*. Rachel stood up and walked slowly to Rusty's office. There was a quiet moment between them as she handed it to him.

Rusty gently took the story from Rachel's hand and said, "This is it, your life-changing story."

"Yes. I've talked to other journalists about this kind of story. They all tell me, 'After writing it I could never go back.' It was like they would forever move in a new direction. I feel as if I've grown a decade in these past few months."

"Your story is going to make an impact on many people. I know it's made an impact on me. I've never thought about dignity issues surrounding death. I can't wait to read this final copy."

"I assume it will go into next week's edition."

"You bet your life on it. Sorry, bad choice of words. Speaking of, is Tim following you home?"

"No, Kyle's picking me up. We're going out to dinner. I may just leave my car here tonight. Would you like to come?"

"No thanks. I'm going to finish some things here. You two deserve a night out. Go have some fun."

Rachel paused and quickly hugged Rusty around the neck as she said, "Thank you, Rusty, for fighting on my behalf. I know your job was on the line."

"Well, I've been fired before. I've survived. But you're welcome."

Just then Kyle walked through Rusty's door and extended a hand to Rusty. "Good to see you, Rusty. You're looking good."

Rusty held up the pages and answered Kyle. "I'm much better now. You're looking pretty fit yourself. Well, you two better get going. Rachel, if you'd like to take a couple of days off, it'd be fine with me."

"You know, I was thinking of doing just that."

Kyle and Rachel sat in a private, romantic booth at their favorite Italian restaurant. The waiter asked in a quiet voice, "Could I get you anything to drink?"

Kyle said, "Yes, a bottle of Merlot please."

"Certainly, and I'll be right back with some of our freshly baked bread."

Kyle smiled at Rachel and took her hand in his. "I'm starving."

"Yeah, me too."

"Hey, I forgot to ask about Senator Green. How's he doing?"

"He's improving today. He has several fractures and a concussion, but he'll make it. I had a call on my answering machine from Senator Price."

"Senator Price? Who's that?"

"Evidently he is a good friend of Senator Green. He said he was calling for Senator Green, gave me a quick update, and asked me to call him back. I didn't get a chance to yet."

"What do you think he wants?"

"I really don't know. Maybe he's just checking on the story. I'll call him from home tomorrow."

"I like that you're going to be home tomorrow. Maybe I can slip home during my break. When do you think we should get the girls?"

"Well, I haven't received any more threatening phone calls, so very soon."

"Okay."

The waiter arrived with the wine and bread. Kyle lifted his glass and said, "What should we drink to?"

Rachel responded, "To life with dignity."

Kyle said as he clinked his glass to Rachel's, "To life with dignity. By the way, Linda has offered to bring the girls back."

Tears came to Rachel's eyes. "Perfect."

The next morning Rachel slept in until nine. She was shocked when she rolled over and looked at the clock. She was on her way to the bathroom when the phone rang. She looked at the caller ID and saw it was her mother.

"Hello."

It was Sarah's voice. "Hi, Mom, are you still sleeping?"

"No, honey, I just haven't had my coffee yet this morning. How are you guys doing?"

"We're fine. We miss you."

"I miss you so much. Did you go to the aquarium?"

"Yep, and we ate at a place called Bubba Gump's. It was fun."

"That sounds great. Dad and I were thinking you should come home soon. What do you think?"

Sarah yelled to her younger sister, "Laura, Mom and Dad want us to come home."

Rachel cut in, "Hey, is Grandma around?"

Sarah dropped the phone and hurried away to find her grandmother. Soon Linda picked up the phone. "Hello, Rachel. So I hear we'll be coming to Phoenix soon. That means you're safe?"

Rachel replied, "Hi, Mom. Yes, I believe the danger's about over. I just want to thank you for everything. The girls seem really happy."

Linda laughed. "They should be. I think we've made up for the past few years."

"I'm glad. Mom, I need to run to the bathroom. Can I call you back with the details?"

"Yes, but are you sure things are safe?"

"I think so. My story's in, so they can't stop that; and

the FBI is investigating Senator Green's hit and run. I don't think they would try anything now."

"Well that's a relief. I've been watching over our shoulders here. Maybe I can relax some now."

"I think you can. I've really got to go, Mom. Call you later."

Rachel spent her morning doing casual housework. She folded clothes and watched one of the cable news broadcasts. She watched as the attractive, blonde newswoman reported that Senator Green continued to improve. Rachel grabbed the remote and turned up the volume.

The newscaster said, "The FBI is in search of a black Toyota Camry with a possible broken taillight. The first three figures of the license plate are B-8–2."

Rachel sat down. She was thankful Senator Green was on the mend but wanted to make sure. She turned off the television and started dialing.

Senator Price's assistant answered.

"Yes, this is Rachel Scott returning Senator Price's call."

"Please hold, Ms. Scott."

The elevator music came on, and Rachel resumed her folding. She wondered if Senator Price would be as nice as Senator Green. Rachel had always thought of politicians as little boys in men's bodies. She was beginning to realize the significance of their work and the impact their decisions could make on everyone's lives.

"Hello, this is John Price. I appreciate you calling me back, Rachel."

"No problem. How's Senator Green?"

"He's a tough cookie. He'll be up and around in no time."

"Do you have any idea who might have done this?"

"Not yet. But I will tell you the FBI has some good leads on the driver. We'll know soon enough. Listen, the reason I called is that Jim, ah Senator Green, asked me to check on your story."

"The story's all wrapped up. It should be in next week's edition."

"Excellent! Senator Green has a timeline for everything. He feels if everything falls into place the impact on Peaceful Transitions could be pretty severe."

"What kind of timeline?"

"I can't really say right now. Would you be willing to attend the Senate hearing with us next month? We'd like you to sit with Senator Green at the table for testimony. You could give special insight."

Rachel smiled broadly as she answered, "Of course, I would be honored. I need to check with my magazine, though."

"I understand. Also, it might be good to have a couple of clients testify. Do you know anyone who might be willing?"

"I might. I'll make some calls and get back to you."

"Thanks. I can't wait to read your story. I'll take a copy to Senator Green. Please call soon to confirm your presence for the Senate hearing."

"I will. Please send my regards to Senator Green."

After she hung up, Rachel took a deep breath and replayed the conversation back in her mind. Then she made another call.

Tim answered, "Hello, Rachel."

"Hello, Tim. Can you do me another favor?"

"Shoot."

"I need the address and phone number for Walter Stafford. He might live in Bend, Oregon, because that's is where Dr. Kramer's practice is located."

"You got it. I'll talk to you soon."

"Thanks. Now I have to call our friend Gerald. I hope he's up for a trip to Washington, DC."

Rachel was excited to have her mom visiting at her house. Rachel had come to terms with Linda's action toward Grandpa James in his last days. Rachel finally realized that she was not responsible for the action of others, nor was it her place to judge or try to change them.

When Linda and the girls opened the door to the house, Rachel greeted them sporting a new haircut. Kyle started gathering suitcases.

Sarah touched her mom's hair and said, "Hi, Mom. Your hair looks great."

Rachel hugged them both tightly. She said, "I had some time off work this week, so I got a haircut."

Laura exclaimed, "Look, I got a tan! We played at a park called Dennis the Menace Park."

Kyle laughed. "Oh really."

Sarah answered, "It's true. It was really called that. Did you go there when you were a kid, Mom?"

"Yes, mostly on field trips with my school."

Linda smiled and said, "Yes, Grandma and Grandpa were very busy back then."

Rachel gave her mother a hug. "It's good to see you, Mom."

Linda pulled back and took a look at her daughter. "I

love your haircut. I wish you would look after yourself more
often."

There was a time Rachel would have taken offense and
snapped at her mother. Now she simply said, "Well, maybe
I will."

Kyle said, "Who wants to help me out back? Mom has
a surprise!"

Laura wasted no time volunteering. "I do, I do!"

Kyle and the two girls went outside. Rachel and Linda
sat down on the sofa.

Linda asked, "So, when do you go back to work?"

"The middle of next week. I have really enjoyed this
time off."

"And I have enjoyed this time with my granddaughters.
Rachel, I know I don't say this enough, and I probably don't
show it either, but I do love you."

"I love you too, Mom."

The girls flew back into the room, Laura holding a beautiful kitten.

14

Linda had only stayed a few days. She somehow could not imagine Carmel going on without her.

Rachel looked in the mirror as she finished getting ready for work. She thought it was ironic that she somehow looked younger but felt older and wiser. She walked down the stairway, and as she entered the kitchen, she saw breakfast on the table. At her place setting sat a vase of beautiful roses. Placed next to the roses was the latest issue of *Situational Life*. The front cover read, *Dignity in Question: Is there ever dignity in death?* There was a picture of an elderly man lying in a hospital bed with an IV attached to his arm.

Kyle said, "Congratulations, honey. We love your story."

Sarah agreed. "Yeah, Mom. You worked really hard on this one."

In a daze, Rachel asked, "How did you get that?"

"Hot off the press. I asked Rusty to arrange an early delivery," said Kyle.

"You are amazing."

Kyle pulled out Rachel's chair and said, "Sit down to breakfast and enjoy the read."

Laura pleaded, "Read it to me, Mom."

Rachel smiled. "Okay, everyone join me for breakfast, and I'll read you my story."

Sarah paused and asked, "It's not a happy story, is it, Mom?"

"No, not so happy, but very hopeful."

As the Scotts ate their breakfast, Rachel began to read her story.

Rachel walked into *Situational Life*'s office building as if floating on air. As she turned the corner, all the staff stood and clapped. There were balloons and a large cake at a table set up near her desk.

Rusty walked slowly toward Rachel and took her hand in his. "Rachel, your story was a beautiful piece of work. The phone has been ringing off the hook."

"You're kidding! What kind of calls?"

"ABC, CNN, Fox, even Oprah Winfrey's people. I have a feeling you better sharpen up your interview skills."

Rachel nervously answered, "What interview skills?"

Everyone laughed as one of Rachel's coworkers pointed at the overhead television and squealed, "Hey, everybody quiet!"

A QUESTION OF DIGNITY

The anchorman on TV stood outside of Peaceful Transitions, and a mob of picketers was expressing its freedom of speech. The anchorman braced himself and began, "This has just transpired within the hour. The crowd is growing with anti-euthanasia protestors. Some of them are chanting, 'Stop the killing.' There is now law enforcement at the scene to control the crowd. We will bring you a complete story at our six p.m. broadcast."

Rusty and Rachel stood staring at each other, too stunned to speak.

Rachel finally broke the silence and said, "I guess it's started."

"It's going to keep building right up to the Senate hearing."

"It'll be a hot topic for a while. Then something new will come along."

"Timing is everything, Rachel. Do what you can now. Don't worry about the rest. Now, relax and enjoy the moment."

Rachel stuck her fork into a piece of cake. She took a bite and said, "Yes, I believe I will!"

It was a busy night at Big Joe's Bar and Grill. Tim and Rusty sat at a table close to an overhead television. There was a pitcher of beer at their table, and both were sipping on their mugs. Finally the anchorperson began interviewing the four panel guests. The distinguished guests were Rachel Scott, Peter Wade, Father Reed, and Laura Lee.

The anchorperson began, "We are going to begin our discussion on euthanasia. With us is Rachel Scott, a writer for *Situational Life* Magazine. Rachel just published a remarkable story on euthanasia and in particular, a glimpse into the practices of Peaceful Transitions. Peaceful Transitions is the first legalized euthanasia clinic in the country. It is located in Portland, Oregon. There has been continuous protest there since the story was published. Rachel, I'd like to start with you. Did you have an opinion on euthanasia before you started your story?"

"On the surface I didn't. It was only after I began researching the clinic that I started to unravel some inner feelings. I believe I remained objective, but the unraveled truth steered me toward some of the clinic's hidden motives."

The anchorperson said "All right. Now I'd like to bring in Peter Wade. Peter is a minister who specializes in grief counseling. Peter, a couple of hidden motives Rachel mentions in her story include greed and desperation. What drives a person to consider and, eventually, choose euthanasia?"

"I believe a big driving factor is a sense of hopelessness, or the fear of being a burden. When people are faced with the reality of imminent death, they become very vulnerable. They can be easily deceived."

Laura Lee interrupted and spoke in a loud voice. "Wait a minute, Peter. Are you saying that people aren't capable of making choices just because they're dying? Our country is about individual choices. What gives the government the right to intervene?"

The anchorperson responded, "That was Laura Lee, an outspoken advocate for euthanasia. I believe Laura was referring to the Senate hearing tomorrow. A special committee was formed to investigate the effects of legalized euthanasia. Now let's hear from Father Lee, a Catholic priest at Sacred

Heart Cathedral. Father, does the Catholic Church support legalized euthanasia?"

"We are against taking lives. Even more than that, as you know, Pope John Paul reversed his position on tube feeding. He feels that removing or refusing this medical intervention is a form of passive euthanasia."

Peter jumped in. "I have to respectfully disagree with Father Reed on one point. Choosing how you wish to live out the rest of your life is clearly different than choosing the exact time and method of your death. In fact, I believe there is no *passive* suicide. There is only active suicide."

Laura Lee answered in disgust, "Peter, you sound awfully judgmental. Again I have to say euthanasia is an individual right."

"It's not about whether a person has a right to end his life. It's about whether or not the states ought to be allowed to support and subsidize euthanasia clinics, especially with the information brought to light in Mrs. Scott's story."

Rachel asked, "May I say something?"

The anchorperson said, "Yes, let's give Rachel an opportunity to speak."

"I believe the case will be made next week in front of the Senate members. Peter is right about the vulnerability of a dying person. Especially with circumstances such as decreased mental capacity, pain, or lack of support. It's about choices but more than just individual. Our society as a whole has a responsibility to decide how we wish to support our terminal population. *Death with dignity* is not about turning a dying society over to a euthanasia clinic. It's about supporting the rest of their lives with a dignified environment."

The anchorperson announced they were out of time. Then

it was announced that the television station would air the Senate session the following week at eleven a.m. eastern time.

Tim and Rusty raised their mugs. Tim said, "Our girl held her own."

Rusty said, "I have a feeling we are just beginning to see the real Rachel. Since her story broke out last week, she has handled the press beautifully."

Tim said, "A thing like this can change a person."

"Yeah, it's amazing how you go through your whole life with something inside of you. Then all of a sudden it just jumps out and stares you in the face. You embrace it and become a new person, or you run like the wind."

"That's true."

"Let me ask you something, Tim. If you were facing that kind of money, would you be able to do the same thing our good doctors have done?"

"No way, José. I have my own demons, but blind greed isn't one of them."

"I've thought about it, and I can't imagine anyone's mind going there."

"That's a good thing. Well, friend, I'm turning into a pumpkin."

Rusty looked at his watch and replied, "Isn't it kind of early to turn into a pumpkin? I thought the magic hour was midnight."

"Not for me. Early to bed, early to rise."

"Well, thanks again for your help."

"My pleasure," said Tim as he left the table.

As Rusty sat alone, he raised his mug and said aloud, smiling, "Here's to you, Rachel."

Rachel stood on her hotel room's balcony in Washington, DC. She reflected on the television interview, hoping she had touched on the points she had wanted. The interview had gone so fast, and the interruptions had taken her by surprise. Even so, she felt peaceful as her hair blew in the wind. Kyle walked up behind Rachel and embraced her, kissing her neck.

"Thinking about tomorrow?"

"Yes, and about public reaction to my story. It's hard to believe there are people who still support the clinic."

"Remember, you can't save the world."

"You're right. I should be thankful for those who are willing to give euthanasia a serious thought."

"Exactly. So what's going on with Dr. McKay's IRS investigation?"

"According to Senator Price, timing is everything. I think there's a carefully orchestrated plan."

"That sounds a little devious."

"No, not really. Look at Esther in the Bible. She carefully planned the demise of Haman. She was led by God and waited for the right time to expose him to the king."

There was a knock on their hotel door. Rachel asked Kyle, "Did you order room service?"

Kyle shrugged his shoulders and smiled at Rachel.

Rachel jogged toward the door. "Good, I could use some food."

Rachel opened the door wide, and to her surprise her mother stood in the doorway. "Mom, what are you doing?"

"What do you think I'm doing? You didn't think I would miss my daughter's big day, did you?"

Rachel turned to Kyle with slanted eyes and asked, "Are you in on this?"

"I thought it would be good for both of us."

"Mom, I'm so glad you came. This is perfect."

"Did I hear you say you could use some food?"

"Yes, you did."

Kyle said, "I'll take care of the food. You two relax and visit."

Kyle called room service while Rachel returned to the balcony with Linda.

Rachel felt as if she had entered a new dimension of her life. She was glad she had pushed through the questions and pain. She never dreamed the efforts could affect so many areas of her life.

Rachel was both nervous and excited on the drive to the United States Capitol. She was greeted by Senator Price upon her arrival to the capitol.

"Hello, Rachel. It's such a pleasure to meet you."

Rachel extended her hand. "Likewise, Senator Price." She turned toward Kyle and Linda. "I'd like to introduce you to my husband, Kyle, and my mother, Linda."

Senator Price greeted them both with a cordial handshake. "Pleasure to meet you both. I'm sure you're very proud of this young lady."

Kyle said, "We are, Senator. She has a special gift."

Linda said, "She didn't get it from me."

They all laughed. Senator Price glanced at his watch.

"Rachel, you'll be called in shortly. I'll take your family in to be seated."

"Thank you." Rachel gave Kyle a quick hug and watched as he and her mother walked down the long hall. Her cell phone rang, and she silently scolded herself for forgetting to turn it off. She looked at the name on the screen and answered.

"Hello, Tim, are you here?"

"You bet. Where are you?"

"I'm waiting on the north side."

"We'll be right there."

Several minutes passed before Rachel spotted the two coming. She walked quickly to greet them.

"Hello, Walter." Rachel embraced Walter, and tears filled her eyes as she thought about their last encounter.

"Hello, Rachel, your story was amazing. I just wish we had known . . ."

"Walter, you didn't know. Gracie knows that. Just remember, you're here now because of what you know, and this is for Gracie."

Rachel and Walter were called into the hearing. They entered the massive room, and sitting before the Senate Committee at a long, rectangular table was Senator Green. At the end of the table sat Dr. McKay and Dr. Kramer. Rachel and Walter took their seats.

Majority Leader Cain opened the meeting. "We will now hear testimony and have questions regarding legalized euthanasia. Specifically, the operation of Peaceful Transitions will be discussed. For those who may not know, Peaceful Transitions is the only legalized euthanasia clinic in the U.S. Senator Green, the committee would like to ask you to start with a short synopsis of why you feel this committee and hearing are needed."

Senator Green was prepared. "Yes, I would like to begin by thanking my distinguished peers for considering this most important matter. I'd like to quickly introduce the individuals sitting with me for testimony. Sitting beside me is Mrs. Scott of *Situational Life* Magazine. I hope all of you had the opportunity to read Rachel's story on Peaceful Transitions. It was an eloquent and brilliant piece of writing. To Rachel's right is Walter Stafford. Walter's wife, Gracie, was a client at Peaceful Transitions. Walter and Gracie were referred to Peaceful Transitions by Dr. Kramer, who is also on the board of directors at Peaceful Transitions. As mentioned in Mrs. Scott's story, there were several patients referred by Dr. Kramer. I know that many of you have reservations about our government getting involved with matters of the individual states. I usually agree that our states should have control over their own functions. But there are times when we are called to oversee certain practices that involve the nation as a whole. I believe this is most definitely one of those times. Thank you."

Majority Leader Cain responded, "Thank you, Senator Green. I'd like to get beginning statements from the other guests then proceed to questions from the Senate commission panel. Mrs. Scott, perhaps you could start."

Rachel looked into the eyes of the panel and began with soft words. "I realized throughout my research on euthanasia how many people choose to die out of fear. I also discovered there are people who will prey on those fears in the worst possible ways. We are here today to talk about an important segment in each and every one of our lives—our final days. Throughout my research I heard terminology such as 'death with dignity' and 'end the suffering.' The truth I came to know is that it is not the terminally ill whose dignity is in question. It is society's. To excuse an act of taking someone's life is an act of deceit. It is deceitful to the terminally ill, cognitively disabled, and to society in general. I recently visited a place for the cognitively impaired; an Alzheimer's facility called New Perceptions. The staff members communicate with the residents on levels beyond reasoning. Beyond the communication is altering the external environment for the residents. It is a beautiful and yes, dignified, world. I have also seen suffering and pain controlled through hospice care. I would like to show you a man named Gerald Sides. Gerald passed away three days ago. He very much wanted to be here today and share his story in person." Rachel looked at Majority Leader Cain and asked, "May we play the tape now?"

Majority Leader Cain agreed, and everyone looked toward the screen. The tape began playing, and Gerald appeared on the screen. The room was silent as the camera zoomed in on Gerald. He was sitting on a recliner chair with a blanket on his lap. He appeared slightly sedated, and his voice was weak but audible. "I would like to thank the distinguished senators for their careful consideration of Senator Green's concern over this country's first euthanasia clinic. I have found in my lifetime that things which are intended to be good can be twisted and turned for evil if society allows. I believe the movement toward advanced directives was indeed a good thing for the dying population. It was designed to give people choices about how they wanted to live out the rest of their days. Then people full of fear, desperation, selfish motives, and even greed were allowed to twist this movement and somehow convince society that planned death was the only way to preserve dignity. I was approached with this concept by my physician, Dr. Kramer, who is also on the board of directors at Peaceful Transitions. When I was suffering with great pain and in a vulnerable state, I was told there was only one dignified solution. It didn't feel right to my soul, and thank God I found the strength to walk away. I can't imagine not having had the past couple of months. I have resolved many things. In my mind there is only one way to die with dignity. That is to face it head on and receive the support of organizations like hospice. I believe I'm experiencing death with dignity now. I would like to close by thanking Senator Green and Rachel Scott. I pray blessings upon you both. Good day."

There wasn't a dry eye left in the place, with the exception of Dr. Kramer and Dr. McKay, who were shifting uncomfortably in their seats. Majority Leader Cain glared at the two of them before shifting his focus to the other side of the panel. "Senator Green, is there another testimony?"

"Yes, we have one more testimony. Mr. Walter Stafford, whose wife, Gracie, was a client of Peaceful Transitions."

Several eyebrows on the Senate panel lifted. Dr. McKay broke out in a sweat and placed his head in his hands.

Majority Leader Cain responded, "Very well, you can proceed, Mr. Stafford."

"Thank you. I've never done anything like this before. It's pretty intimidating. Gracie and I weren't as lucky or wise as Gerald there. We bought all the smooth talk and went through with it. We were also referred by Dr. Kramer. Now that I look back, I can see that Gracie didn't want me to feel burdened. She always took care of me. Like Gerald, Gracie was also afraid. But Gracie was not afraid for herself. She was afraid for me. And I was afraid too. I was afraid to see her suffer. I had heard of hospice but didn't really know what the services were. In retrospect I should have picked up the phone and called them myself."

Tears began to swell in Walter's eyes. He reached into his coat pocket and lifted out a white handkerchief with pink embroidering. It was Gracie's. Walter continued, "There is not a second of a day that goes by that I don't regret what happened to Gracie. We were married when we were seventeen. We were blessed with two wonderful children. They're both still in shock over this. I know they forgive me and love me, but I don't think they'll ever get over this. I don't know if it makes a difference, but it cost us ten thousand dollars to end Gracie's life. Today I'd give every single thing I own just to have Gracie back for her intended time, whether it would be for three days, three weeks, or three months. That's all I can say. Thank you."

Senator Green said, "Thank you, Walter. Majority Leader, we welcome any questions you might have at this time."

"I think I'd like to hear from Doctors Kramer and McKay first. Dr. McKay, would you please explain to this panel how Peaceful Transitions was created?"

Dr. McKay cleared his throat. "Yes, of course. I've been practicing geriatric medicine for over twenty-five years. I've been an advocate of euthanasia for most of my professional career. I testified before the Oregon state committee in support of legalizing euthanasia. I have seen my patients and their families over the years suffer and seek a way out. Euthanasia is the most compassionate intervention for dying patients, especially for those who have lost hope or experience uncontrollable pain.

"I still believe that a person has a right to choice. And a caregiver should have that right also. It is wrong for the Senate and Congress to get involved. This should be left up to the individual states. I hope the Senate members will leave things as they are. Things are progressing forward, and there is no need to take this big step back. I'm sorry for the families that are unable to accept the deaths of their loved ones. But there are many families at peace with euthanasia intervention. Thank you for your time."

Majority Leader Cain looked to Dr. Kramer and asked, "Dr. Kramer, do you have anything to add?"

"You bet I do. I would like to assure the panel that at no time did I try to force this option upon my patients. It has always simply been an alternative. They made the choice of euthanasia of their own free will. That is all."

Several of the Senate members began to look around at each other. Majority Leader Cain directed his next question to Senator O'Connor. "What is your take on Peaceful Transitions?"

"Thank you, Majority Leader Cain. The people of my state strongly support individual choice. In addition, we strongly adhere to a budget so that taxes can be kept as low as possible. We recognize it is the state's responsibility to care for our indigent, but we realistically cannot pick up the tab that the federal government has failed to carry. With the baby boomers here and absolutely no long-term-care financial system in place for the elderly, we simply are facing a crisis. When our elderly and terminally ill people reach a point of overwhelming burden, the people of our state support legalized euthanasia."

Majority Leader Cain scowled. "I think some of my colleagues may have a few questions. I know I do." He turned to Senator Hufford and asked, "Senator Hufford, would you start us off?"

Senator Hufford had been representing North Carolina for twelve years. He was now sixty years old and well respected and rooted in the Senate. He began to speak in his strong southern accent. "Dr. Kramer, you say you only presented euthanasia as an option. But aren't you on the board of directors at Peaceful Transitions? Wouldn't you consider this to be a conflict of interest?"

"No, I wouldn't, Senator Hufford. I'm an experienced geriatric physician. I feel my experience brought a lot of knowledge to the board."

"Okay then, but I still feel like a conflict of interest exists here. I would like to ask Dr. McKay, where are the family members you mentioned were at peace with euthanasia interventions? Surely you could have found one or two that would testify today."

Dr. McKay cleared his throat and sputtered, "We felt that asking our clients to testify could cause our families to have a setback in their grieving processes. We just didn't want to exploit their grief."

"Well, you do understand this committee has serious doubts about what is going on at your facility. It seems you would be more vigilant in stating your case. Ms. Scott, I have a question for you. In your story on Peaceful Transitions, you mention that the clinic receives quite a substantial income for its services. Did you discover the exact amount? If so I would like to hear it."

"Yes, I did obtain a copy of last year's filed taxes. However, there may be some discrepancy in the amount. The amount of net intake for last year is 480,000 dollars."

"Do you have a copy of that return with you?"

"Yes, I do."

"I'd like to see it. In fact I'm sure all of us would." Senator Hufford looked around the committee to see the panel nodding. Dr. Kramer looked as if someone had hit him in the stomach with a sledgehammer.

Senator Hufford continued, "I just have one more question for Senator O'Connor. Senator, in your opening statement, it sounded like a lack of financial resources was your state's justification for legalized euthanasia. But doesn't your state financially support Peaceful Transitions?"

"Yes, but the cost is minimal compared to a long-term care situation. The cost of long-term placement is extensive. I don't think you can even compare the two. But I want to be clear that financial burden is not the justification for my state's legalization of euthanasia."

"Well, what is it?"

"We support individual choice. Each person has a right to do what he wishes with his own body."

"I have no other questions."

Senator Price was the next person on the committee to speak. "Dr. McKay, I have a copy of your last year's IRS returns. I also have a copy of your bank statements. I obtained these records through the Federal Bureau of Investigations. I want to assure the committee that appropriate subpoenas, etc., were obtained to get these records. Would you like to explain, Dr. McKay, why over a million dollars of income was not reported on your tax return?"

Heads turned to Dr. McKay as the panel waited for an answer.

"I don't know what you're referring to, Senator Price."

Senator Price pressed on. "I'm referring to an offshore account that makes you a millionaire."

"That money is from a source other than Peaceful Transitions."

"Dr. McKay, maybe you aren't clear on this. The FBI has conducted a thorough investigation into your clinic. Now the books are not adding up. So go ahead and explain your other source if you can."

Dr. McKay and Dr. Kramer began to whisper to one another. Senator Price raised his voice an octave. "Dr. McKay, my time is limited, so please answer my question now."

"I wish to take the fifth on this matter. I'd like to consult my lawyer."

"I expect you do. And believe me, Dr. McKay, you're going to need a lawyer."

The room was completely silent, and Senator Green was slightly smiling. Senator Price said, "It seems Dr. McKay has nothing to say, so I'm finished."

Majority Leader Cain spoke up. "I believe this should conclude the Senate hearing on legalized euthanasia. I would like to thank the Senate panel, Senator Green, and the guests who gave testimony. The results of our investigation will be available in a few weeks."

The meeting was adjourned, and Rachel immediately exchanged a long hug with Walter. "Thank you, Walter."

"Mrs. Scott, believe me when I say that the honor was mine."

Senator Green shook Rachel's hand then Walter's.

Rachel said, "I see what you mean about timing. What happens next?"

Senator Green replied, "The Feds are waiting outside. Dr. McKay will be taken into custody. I believe he'll soon be connected to my hit and run."

Rachel stared right into Senator Green's eyes as she responded, "I have to say that I don't feel sorry for him."

"No, Rachel, he made his own bed."

Kyle and Linda had made their way to Rachel. Kyle spoke with pride. "Great job, you guys. You couldn't have presented a better case."

Senator Green smiled and said, "I must get going. I wouldn't want to miss the big moment."

Senator Green opened his walker and started toward the door.

Kyle looked at Rachel and asked, "What big moment?"

Rachel took Kyle's hand. "Let's head outside. Perhaps we'll see."

Rachel, Kyle, and Linda made their way to the outside of the capitol building. On steps outside stood a crowd of reporters moving toward Senator Green. Senator Green started answering questions but was looking around for something or someone.

From the other side of the building, Dr. McKay and Dr. Kramer emerged. Two tall, well-built men in suits walked up to the doctors and announced, "Dr. McKay, we're federal agents, and you are under arrest for the crime of embezzlement and IRS fraud."

One of the agents began to read Dr. McKay his rights. Dr. Kramer looked as if he was about to wet his pants. "Don't say a word, Bill. I'll get our lawyer on the phone right now. Just remain calm."

The federal agents escorted Dr. McKay down the steps and into a dark sedan. Reporters swarmed the car, yelling questions to the men inside. The reporters then spotted Rachel and moved in unison toward her. Questions begin to fire in her direction.

15

Rachel, Kyle, Sarah, and Laura were playing their favorite board game on the coffee table of their living room. The TV was tuned at a low volume to Fox News. Rachel looked up at the television and saw a just-in bulletin on the Senate hearing decision on legalized euthanasia. She grabbed the remote and turned up the volume. As the anchorwoman talked, the picture showed Peaceful Transitions and equipment being moved out of the clinic. The anchorwoman began, "This is Susie John. Just in is the final Senate report on legalized euthanasia. The panel passed a decision stating that legalized euthanasia needs to have more restrictions and guidelines before being considered. Evidently there is some talk of a possible proposal for a federal ban of euthanasia. Currently Oregon has been the only state to legalize euthanasia and support the first euthanasia clinic. Just recently, Washington has joined Oregon in legalizing euthanasia. Now this clinic, called Peaceful Transitions, has been the subject of recent controversy. Rachel Scott of *Situational Life* Magazine brought to light several alarming issues regarding the clinic and testified at last month's Senate hearing. The clinic's director, Dr. McKay, was arrested for IRS fraud and embezzlement. He has been waiting for the preliminary hearing on those charges. It has just been reported that this morning additional charges were filed against Dr. McKay and another physician named Dr. Kramer. Those charges are conspiracy to commit murder against Senator Green. Evidently the person responsible for the hit and run was arrested and took a plea bargain in exchange for naming the person who had hired him. It is reported that Peaceful Transitions is being closed down at this moment. We'll have a full panel of discussions at four o'clock on *Politics Now*. We'll be right back."

Rachel turned down the volume and smiled at Kyle. He winked at her and rolled the dice. They landed right on the game board's name. It read, *LIFE*.